TOURIST TRAP . . .

"Uncle!" Alice cried shrilly.

The outlaw jerked her closer to him. "You shut up!" he snapped. "I don't like no gal screamin' in my ear less'n I'm pleasurin' her. Now come along with me!"

"Please . . . you can't . . ." Sir Harry muttered. He was still stunned by the pistol-whipping he'd received.

The outlaw ignored him and started backing toward the door at the rear of the car. Longarm called after him, "I'll see you again, old son."

"The hell you will," grated the outlaw. "I've decided I don't want a gent like you on my backtrail."

He thrust his gun out, aiming directly at Longarm . . .

DON'T MISS THESE
ALL-ACTION WESTERN SERIES
FROM THE BERKLEY PUBLISHING GROUP

THE GUNSMITH by J. R. Roberts
Clint Adams was a legend among lawmen, outlaws, and ladies.
They called him . . . the Gunsmith.

LONGARM by Tabor Evans
The popular long-running series about U.S. Deputy Marshal
Long—his life, his loves, his fight for justice.

SLOCUM by Jake Logan
Today's longest-running action Western. John Slocum rides
a deadly trail of hot blood and cold steel.

BUSHWHACKERS by B. J. Lanagan
An action-packed series by the creators of Longarm! The
rousing adventures of the most brutal gang of cutthroats ever
assembled—Quantrill's Raiders.

DIAMONDBACK by Guy Brewer
Dex Yancey is Diamondback, a southern gentleman turned
con man when his brother cheats him out of the family fortune. Ladies love him. Gamblers hate him. But nobody pulls
one over on Dex . . .

WILDGUN by Jack Hanson
Will Barlow's continuing search for his daughter, kidnapped
by the Blackfeet Indians who slaughtered the rest of his family.

TABOR EVANS

LONGARM

AND THE GOLDEN GODDESS

JOVE BOOKS, NEW YORK

LONGARM AND THE GOLDEN GODDESS

A Jove Book / published by arrangement with
the author

PRINTING HISTORY
Jove edition / August 2000

The Penguin Putnam Inc. World Wide Web site address is
http://www.penguinputnam.com

ISBN: 0-515-12890-2

A JOVE BOOK®
Jove Books are published by The Berkley Publishing Group,
a division of Penguin Putnam Inc.,
375 Hudson Street, New York, New York 10014.
JOVE and the "J" design
are trademarks belonging to Penguin Putnam Inc.

PRINTED IN THE UNITED STATES OF AMERICA

10 9 8 7 6 5 4 3 2 1

Chapter 1

Now, that was one fine, firm, well-rounded female rump, Longarm thought. Just looking at it made a fella want to reach out with both hands and cup those inviting cheeks so that he could knead and caress them, maybe even lean over and plant a kiss on each of them in turn. Of course, he'd look mighty silly if he did that in front of all these people, Longarm told himself.

Not to mention the fact that the gal's backside wasn't even real, warm, human flesh, but instead was made of cold, hard stone.

Longarm looked down at the brightly polished tile floor, cleared his throat, and moved on with the rest of the group. As he passed the statue, he thought about giving it a pat on the butt, but he decided that would be foolish too. Besides, one of the museum guards was giving him the skunk-eye. It really wouldn't do for one of Uncle Sam's lawmen to get thrown out of a museum for lecherously fondling a piece of sculpture.

Longarm sighed. So far the job hadn't been as bad as he'd feared it would be, but he wished Billy Vail had picked someplace else for him to meet Sir Harry Black-street.

Sir Harry was up ahead with Miss Alice Channing on his arm. Alice looked lovely, Longarm thought. She was a whole heap prettier than any statue, in the opinion of United States Deputy Marshal Custis Long, who considered himself sort of an expert when it came to pretty gals. Blackstreet claimed that Alice was his niece, and Alice likely went along with that fiction, but Longarm was convinced that she was his mistress. If that was indeed the case, it had to be because Sir Harry was rich. He wasn't the ugliest gent Longarm had ever seen, but he hadn't attracted a woman like Alice with his looks.

They made a pretty odd pair, Longarm mused. Sir Harry was a big man, only a couple of inches shorter than Longarm, with broad shoulders and a massive belly. He was mostly bald, having only a fringe of white hair around his ears and the back of his head. His clean-shaven face was as pink as a baby's, and also like a baby—a well-fed baby—he sported a pair of chins. His eyes were deep-set in pits of gristle beneath bushy white eyebrows. He smiled frequently, but even though Longarm had met him only a short time earlier, he had already figured out that Sir Harry Blackstreet's smiles rarely made it from his mouth to those dark, intelligent eyes.

Miss Alice Channing, on the other hand, was quite petite, and appeared even more so when she stood next to the massive Blackstreet. Her blonde hair was cut short and swept in two wings around her lovely face. She wore a dark blue gown and a matching hat with a little feather on it. The dress was tight enough to reveal that while she might be small, she wasn't some dainty little doll. The curves of her body were plenty womanly, and as Longarm followed along behind them, he found himself wondering just how well Alice's rump would compare with the backside of that statue he had been looking at a few minutes earlier. He suspicioned that the real thing would stand up just fine.

Sir Harry paused in front of a painting. He turned toward Longarm, grunted, and said, "Exquisite brushwork, don't you think, Marshal?"

Longarm, whose most extensive exposure to painting had come complete with a horsehair brush, a bucket of white-wash, and the raw planks of a country church back in West-by-God Virginia when he was a youngster, just nodded and said, "I suppose so."

"And look at the composition," Sir Harry went on. "Quite daring, wouldn't you say?"

All Longarm saw in the painting was a sissified-looking gent standing next to a table with a vase of flowers on it, while a woman sat behind the table in a chair. The woman wasn't nearly as pretty as Alice Channing either. But Long-arm nodded anyway in response to Sir Harry's question and said, "I reckon."

Sir Harry gave him one of those mouth-only smiles, and Longarm figured the Englishman thought he was nothing but an uncultured, ignorant boor. That was all right with Longarm. Let Blackstreet think whatever he wanted.

He would do well to remember, though, that the only reason Longarm was here was to protect him.

"Why don't we move along, Sir Harry?" the museum curator suggested. He and several members of Denver's high society were accompanying Sir Harry and his "niece" on this tour of Denver's newly opened art museum. It was located in what had been a private mansion belonging to one of the gold and silver barons, not far from the famed Opera House. The owner of the mansion had died and left the place to the city, along with his collection of paintings and sculpture, with the proviso that Denver's city fathers would not only maintain the collection but would also add to it. A lot of folks who lived in Denver now prided them-selves on its culture, preferring to forget about the rough-and-tumble origins of the city, so they'd hired some college professor from back East to come out and run the museum. The hope was that the museum would attract the right kind of visitors to the city.

Longarm supposed Sir Harry Blackstreet fit into that cat-egory, since he was a visiting British nobleman and all. The locals were even willing to accept that cock-and-bull

3

story about Alice being Blackstreet's niece as long as it meant they, and the museum, got a good write-up in the society pages of the Denver newspapers.

As he trooped along after the bunch, Longarm couldn't help but sigh and wish he had been somewhere else this morning when Billy Vail had stepped out of the chief marshal's office in Denver's Federal Building.

Longarm stretched his legs out in front of him, cocked one ankle over the other, and tilted up the cheroot clenched between his teeth at a jaunty angle. He started to hum a little tune.

Henry, the mousy little fella who played the typewriter in Billy Vail's outer office, looked at Longarm over the spectacles perched on the end of his nose and said, "Must you do that?"

"Do what?" Longarm asked innocently as he took the cheroot out of his mouth.

"Make that noise," snapped Henry.

"What noise?"

"You're . . . humming, I suppose you'd call it. Either that, or choking to death."

"Oh," Longarm said. "Well, I'll sure try to stop that, Henry."

Henry just glared at him and went back to what he was doing, which as far as Longarm could tell consisted of moving papers from one stack to another, then moving them back again. After a moment Longarm began drumming his fingers on the wooden arm of the chair where he was sitting.

It didn't take long for Henry to say, "*Now* what are you doing?"

Longarm looked down at his hand as if he had never seen it before, then moved it from the arm of the chair to his lap. "Sorry," he said contritely.

Henry snorted and looked as if he didn't believe a word of it. Longarm leaned back, puffed on the cheroot, and blew a perfect smoke ring.

4

Damn, he was bored! Twitting Henry like that was proof of it. If he didn't have anything better to do than deliberately annoy the little fella—

The door of Billy Vail's private office was jerked open, and the chief marshal himself stepped out hurriedly. He looked around the outer office, and his eyes fell on Longarm, lounging beside the door. "Custis!" he barked. "Get in here."

Oh, Lordy, Longarm thought. He should have gotten out while the getting was good.

He unfolded his tall, rangy frame from the chair. Consistent with the regulations of the United States Justice Department, he was wearing a suit, his usual brown tweed outfit with a vest, white shirt, and black string tie. A gold watch chain looped across his chest from one vest pocket to the other. At one end of the chain was a heavy gold pocket watch, as anyone would expect to find. Welded to the other end of the chain was the butt of a two-shot .44 derringer that had saved Longarm's bacon on more than one occasion. Since he was indoors, Longarm wasn't wearing his flat-crowned, snuff-brown Stetson, but carrying it instead. That left his thatch of dark brown hair uncovered. His sweeping longhorn mustache was the same color. His face was tanned like saddle leather, and his high cheekbones made him appear to have a touch of Indian blood in him, when in fact he didn't have a drop. He was in the prime of life, a tough, experienced manhunter who knew how to use the Colt .44 revolver he carried in a cross-draw rig on his left hip, under the suit coat. As he followed Vail into the inner office, he asked hopefully, "What've you got for me, Billy? Counterfeiters, train robbers, something like that?"

Vail went behind his document-covered desk and said, "I want you to get over to that new art museum here in town."

Longarm tried not to gape at his pudgy, pink-cheeked boss. "Art museum?" he repeated slowly.

"That's right." Vail sat down and motioned for Longarm

5

to have a seat in the red leather chair in front of the desk. He picked up a sheaf of papers and tossed them to the front edge of the desk. "Take a look at those."

As he sat down, Longarm picked up the papers and quickly scanned the writing on the top sheet. It was a report from the Chicago police, he saw, concerning an attempted robbery in their fair city. The victim, or almost victim, had been a visiting Englishman named Sir Harry Blackstreet. According to the report, several men had accosted Blackstreet and his niece on the street as they left their hotel. Blackstreet had fought back, guns had been pulled, and somebody probably would have been badly hurt, even killed, if not for the timely intervention of the hotel doorman and a nearby police officer. Blackstreet had been shaken up but not really injured, and his niece had been badly frightened.

It took less than a minute for Longarm to glean that information from the report. He went on to the next sheet, which was a report of a similar crime. This report, however, came from the headquarters of the Denver & Rio Grande Railroad. Once again, robbers had targeted Sir Harry Blackstreet, this time as he and his niece rode the train between Chicago and Denver. The thieves had been no more successful on this second attempt, if indeed they were the same men, as Blackstreet swore they were. A couple of porters on the train had come to Blackstreet's aid, and the robbers had been forced to jump from the train as it slowed for a grade.

The second attempt had been enough to convince Blackstreet he was in danger, so at the next stop, he had telegraphed the British embassy in Washington and requested assistance. The British embassy had contacted the U.S. State Department, which had in turn contacted the Justice Department. And as usual, when somebody in Washington hollered for help, Billy Vail answered.

Which dumped the whole thing squarely in his lap, Longarm reasoned. He grimaced.

"Don't like the looks of it, eh?" Vail asked.

"Dang it, Billy, the last time you set me to riding herd on a stray Englishman, down in the Sangre de Cristos, I almost got killed!" Longarm exclaimed.

"But you didn't," Vail pointed out. "And you impressed Sir Alfred so much he wrote a letter to the Justice Department telling them what a fine lawman you are. Naturally, they asked me to have this case assigned to you if you were available."

Grimly, Longarm flipped to the next document in the stack. It was a brief biography of Sir Harry Blackstreet. According to the paper, Blackstreet had served in the British Army during the Crimean War and distinguished himself with his "valourous behaviour." After his retirement from the military, he had become a successful financier, and was currently a partner in a British syndicate that owned several lucrative mines in Nevada's Comstock Lode. His current tour of the American West was his first visit to the United States. Traveling with him, Longarm already knew from the other reports, was his niece, Miss Alice Channing.

Longarm looked up at Vail. "Blackstreet says the same fellas jumped him and his niece both times."

"That's right," Vail agreed with a nod. He seemed to be waiting for Longarm to say something else.

Longarm obliged by thinking out loud. "Then they must be after something in particular."

"Maybe they were mad because Blackstreet got away from them in Chicago and decided to follow him to get even."

Vail was just playing the devil's advocate, Longarm thought. He said, "Not likely. I ain't an expert on Chicago crooks, Billy, but I reckon most of 'em got better things to do than go chasing after some fella they didn't get to rob."

"You're right," conceded Vail. "I think they're after something too. But Blackstreet says he doesn't have any idea what it could be."

"You've talked to him?"

Vail nodded. "Last night at his hotel. His train got in late yesterday afternoon, and I'd gotten a wire earlier in the day from Washington instructing me to talk to him. He claims there's no reason for a band of highwaymen, as he put it, to be after him."

Longarm put the documents on the desk and tapped them with a blunt fingertip. "Says here he's rich. Most thieves are after money. Maybe they really meant to kidnap him and hold him for ransom."

"That's one possibility."

Longarm shook his head and said, "I can't think of another."

"Neither can I, right now," Vail admitted. "All I know for sure is that Blackstreet and his niece are going to be visiting the art museum. You can start the job there. Stick to him like a burr."

"For how long?"

"Until he's out of Denver anyway. He's bound for Nevada, plans to visit those mines his company owns out there, but we'll decide later if you need to go all the way to Nevada with him."

Longarm nodded. This job was shaping up to be more interesting than he had thought when Vail fist presented it. As a rule, Longarm didn't like bodyguard assignments. He preferred to be out tracking down the owlhoots, rather than waiting for them to come to him. But he could understand why the bureaucrats in Washington didn't want a fancy foreigner like Sir Harry Blackstreet to be kidnapped while he was on American soil. *If* that was what was really going on here. That hadn't been established yet, Longarm reminded himself.

Still, there were things he didn't like about the job. "Are you sure I couldn't just wait for the gent back at his hotel, Billy?"

"You head on over to the art museum," Vail said firmly. "I was waiting for these reports to get here this morning before I called you in, but now that they have, I want you on the job as soon as possible."

"If I hadn't been here, you'd have given the chore to

8

somebody else, wouldn't you?" Longarm asked.

"Maybe. Time's a-wastin'."

Longarm stood up and put his hat on. "Well, th n, I reckon I'll go soak up some culture."

It didn't take him long to walk from the Federal Building to the museum. When he got there, he was stopped at the front door by a guard in a billed cap and a uniform that looked vaguely like a Denver policeman's uniform. "Closed to the public right now, mister," the guard told him, holding up a hand as if anxious to plant it in the middle of Longarm's chest and shove.

"I ain't the public, old son," Longarm told him, taking out the leather folder that contained his badge and bona fides. "I'm Deputy Marshal Custis Long, and I'm here on business."

The guard didn't seem overly impressed, but he moved out of the way. "If you're looking for the curator, he's taking a private tour through the museum right now, but he'll be free in a little while."

"It's that private tour I'm trying to catch up with," Longarm replied as he moved past the guard and tucked away his identification. His footsteps echoed hollowly in the high-ceilinged foyer. He heard voices and followed them.

The rooms of the museum still looked something like the rooms of a private home. Some of the furniture was still in place: a fancy divan here, an overstuffed armchair there. But the walls were all hung with paintings, and statues filled the corners and alcoves. Most of the statues were of naked people, Longarm realized after a few moments. He supposed nudity equaled art. He had seen some gals in his time who were certainly works of art with all their clothes off.

There were eight or nine people in the group when he caught up to them. The biggest one turned out to be Sir Harry Blackstreet himself, and he shook Longarm's hand heartily, enfolding it with fingers as long and thick as sausages. "So very glad to meet you," he'd said. "Kindly allow me to introduce you to my niece and traveling companion, Miss Alice Channing."

Longarm couldn't have said how he knew it, but he knew right away that Alice wasn't Sir Harry's niece. That left only one logical explanation as to her true identity. Maybe it was the way Blackstreet's hand rested so possessively on her shoulder, or the glint in his dark eyes as he gazed at her. No uncle looked at a niece like that unless he had something in mind that was immoral, illegal, and downright sordid.

Alice took Longarm's hand and murmured that she was pleased to meet him. He said, "Same here, ma'am," then turned back to Sir Harry and began, "Chief Marshal Vail sent me here to—"

Blackstreet waved one of those hamlike hands. "Oh, I know very well why you're here, Marshal. You've been sent to apprehend the miscreants who tried to rob us in Chicago and on the train if they make another attempt to, how do you say it, hold us up."

Longarm didn't want to go into the kidnapping theory with the museum curator and the other society mucky-mucks standing there, so he just nodded and said, "That's right."

"Well, I'm certain you'll be more than a match for them if they're unwise enough to show up here in Denver." Blackstreet nodded to the curator. "Shall we resume the tour?"

That was what they'd been doing for the past thirty minutes, wandering through the numerous rooms of the mansion while the curator talked about the paintings and sculpture and Blackstreet exclaimed delightedly over many of the items. Longarm thought some of the statues were all right, but most of the paintings struck him as too prissy. He'd seen better pictures hanging behind the bar in some of the saloons he'd been in.

The tour was finally over. No trouble had cropped up, but that didn't come as a surprise to Longarm. Whoever was after Sir Harry wouldn't be likely to jump him in the middle of a well-guarded museum. As they left the mansion and stepped out onto the wide porch, Blackstreet said to Longarm, "I assume you'll be accompanying us back to the hotel, Marshal?"

"My boss told me to stick to you like a burr," Longarm said.

Sir Harry was holding a silk top hat that had been collapsed for easier carrying. With a flick of his wrist, he snapped it open and put it on his head, then looped his arm through Alice's. "Come along, my dear." They started down the steps.

A high hedge ran along the sidewalk in front of the mansion, partially blocking the view from the street. Longarm heard the clatter of hooves and wagon wheels on the paving stones, though, and something about the sound made him tense. A moment later, he wasn't particularly surprised when several men stepped around the corners of the mansion and leveled pistols at them. Alice let out a startled cry and shrank against Blackstreet's side.

"All right, fat man," one of the gunmen grated. "You're comin' with us."

Longarm said calmly, "These the same gents as before, Sir Harry?"

Blackstreet sounded genuinely puzzled as he said, "I've never seen these brigands before in my life."

Longarm was surprised too. Whatever was going on, somebody new was horning in on it.

Chapter 2

There were five gunmen, Longarm saw. Three of them were dressed in rough range clothes, while the other two wore the cheap suits and derby hats of townies. All of them could have used a shave. They were tough-looking men. One of them jabbed the barrel of his gun at Blackstreet and said harshly, "Didn't you hear me, you tub of lard? We got a wagon on the street. Get your fat carcass in it!"

Sir Harry glowered at the man. "There's no call to be insulting!" he fumed.

Longarm glanced over at the museum guard who'd tried to stop him from entering the place earlier. The man was the only one of the guards out here; the curator and the other society types had stayed inside too. So if anybody was going to stop this kidnapping, it would have to be Longarm and this lone guard.

Not that Longarm wanted the guard to make any sort of play. That might get them all killed. Longarm wanted to bide his time, at least for a few moments, and wait for a better chance to turn the tables on these desperadoes.

Alice didn't give him a chance to do that. She screamed at the top of her lungs, an ear-piercing shriek that was loud enough and shrill enough to shatter glass, Longarm thought as he muttered, "Shit!" and reached for his gun. That scream would draw plenty of attention and force the gunmen to act. Longarm hoped that museum guard was packing iron somewhere under that fancy uniform.

As Longarm flung himself to the right, Sir Harry swept Alice behind him with an arm like the trunk of a small tree. You couldn't fault the man's personal courage. He bellowed and charged at the nearest of the gunmen. The man looked surprised that Blackstreet was attacking him, but that didn't stop his finger from tightening on the trigger of his Colt.

Longarm shot that fella first, figuring he was the biggest threat to Sir Harry's life. Longarm triggered the shot as he was falling, so his aim was a little off. Instead of drilling the man in the chest, the slug went into his belly, doubling him over in agony. The man's finger clenched involuntarily on the trigger of the gun in his hand, but the shot went into the ground only a couple of feet in front of him.

By then, Longarm was sprawled on his belly on the porch of the museum. He fired again, narrowly missing the man who had ordered Blackstreet to get in the wagon. The man ducked instinctively, so that Longarm's next shot, triggered quickly, caught him in the head. The impact of the bullet boring through his skull and brain sent the man flipping backward like a circus acrobat.

Shots rang out from the other side of the porch, and when Longarm glanced in that direction, he saw that the museum guard was indeed armed. He was firing a short-barreled Colt Lightning toward the remaining gunmen, who threw lead back at him. The guard staggered as a slug thudded into his body, but he didn't go down. He stayed stubbornly on his feet and fired two more shots, sending one of the gunmen spinning to the ground.

Longarm rolled over and came to his feet as a bullet chipped stone from the porch where he had been a second earlier. He fired the last two bullets in the .44's cylinder and had the satisfaction of seeing one of the gunmen stagger back and clutch his chest. The man tried to lift his gun for a final shot before he collapsed, but he didn't make it.

That left only one of the would-be kidnappers, and Sir Harry Blackstreet was taking care of him, Longarm saw. Sir Harry had gotten hold of the man, knocked the gun aside, and snatched him into a bear hug. Blackstreet's left hand was locked around his right wrist in the small of the man's back as he heaved upward. The gunman's feet came up off the ground, and there was a loud snap. The gunman threw his head back and screamed. Sir Harry released the bear hug and brought the heel of his right hand up under the man's uptilted chin. A short, hard shove drove the man's head back even more, and there was another popping noise, this one softer. When Blackstreet stepped back, the man crumpled limply to the ground like a carelessly discarded rag doll.

Longarm had seen men kill other men with their bare hands before, but seldom had he seen the grisly feat performed so quickly and efficiently as Sir Harry Blackstreet had just done it.

Alice had sunk into a huddled heap on the steps of the museum. Longarm moved quickly to her side and looked her over for any signs of injury. There was no blood on her gown. She had both hands pressed to her mouth and was looking wide-eyed at the carnage spread out in front of her. She flinched a little when Longarm put his left hand on her right shoulder.

"You all right, ma'am?" he asked.

Alice turned her head and looked up at him. "Are . . . are they all dead?"

"Seem to be," Longarm replied. "None of those bullets flying around got you, ma'am?"

She responded with a jerky shake of her head. "N-no, I'm fine. Just . . . just frightened."

Longarm couldn't blame her for that. He'd been a mite nervous for a minute there himself. He patted Alice reassuringly on the shoulder, then went to check on the guard, who had finally sagged into a sitting position. There was a dark stain on the man's uniform coat.

"How bad are you hit?" Longarm asked the man as he knelt beside him.

The guard was pale but composed. He shook his head and said, "Not too bad. Bullet knocked a hunk out of my side."

"You did a good job," Longarm told him. "We'll get a sawbones for you and get you to the hospital."

"That'll be . . . fi—" Before he could finish his sentence, the guard's eyes rolled up and he fell over backward. Longarm caught his shoulders and lowered him gently to the surface of the porch. Probably passed out from loss of blood, he thought.

Now that the shooting was all over, the guards from inside the museum came pouring out, followed cautiously by the curator. "My God!" the man exclaimed. "What happened?"

"Some fellas tried to grab Sir Harry," Longarm said. That reminded him of his primary responsibility, and he turned quickly to the visiting British nobleman.

Blackstreet was helping Alice to her feet. He appeared to be unscathed. In fact, he seemed rather proud of himself. When he noticed Longarm looking at him, he said, "My word, that was the first time I've had the opportunity to test myself in personal combat in quite some time. How invigorating!"

"I thought you fought off those gents who jumped you in Chicago and on the train."

Blackstreet shrugged his massive shoulders. "They did not put up a fight the way these fellows did. I haven't heard the siren song of bullets around my head since Balaclava."

That was a song Longarm would just as soon not hear, but Blackstreet seemed to have enjoyed it. Dryly, Longarm said, "You know you killed that hombre, don't you?"

"He was trying to kill me," Sir Harry shot back.

Longarm didn't know if that was strictly true or not. The man he'd gutshot was the only one who had really had a chance to shoot Sir Harry. The other gunmen had been too busy trading shots with Longarm and the museum guard.

15

But there had been enough lead flying around so that the Englishman could have easily been hit. Obviously, while the gunmen had wanted to take him prisoner, it hadn't mattered all that much to them if he wound up dead instead.

That sort of made the kidnapping theory less likely, Longarm thought with a frown.

He'd have to sort that out later, he decided. He moved to Sir Harry's side and said, "We'd better get you back to your hotel."

Sir Harry looked at the passed-out guard. "But that gentleman requires medical attention."

"I've already sent one of the other guards for a doctor and an ambulance," the museum curator said. "We'll see that he's taken care of."

"Well, then . . . Goodness, I've dropped my hat." Sir Harry bent with a grunt and picked up the silk topper from the ground where it had fallen when he'd charged the gunman like a maddened bull. He put it on and adjusted it carefully, then took Alice's arm. "Come along, my dear."

Longarm fell in step behind them. He wanted to get in front in case of more trouble, but for the moment Sir Harry's bulk blocked him.

A groan made him stop. He looked down and saw that the man he'd shot in the belly had started to stir around. The man must have passed out from the shock of the wound, but now he was regaining consciousness. Longarm felt a twinge of sympathy for him. Owlhoot or not, dying from a belly wound was a hell of a bad way to go.

"Wasn't . . . wasn't supposed to . . ." the man gasped. He twisted his head and looked up at Longarm. His mouth opened and closed a couple of times, and he seemed to be trying desperately to tell the lawman something.

"Hold on a minute," Longarm said to Sir Harry and Alice. He went to one knee beside the mortally wounded gunman and said, "What is it?"

"D-didn't tell us . . ." the man said, his voice growing thicker as blood filled his lungs and throat. "Damn . . . double-cr—"

16

His head fell to the side and his eyes closed. Longarm checked the pulse in his neck, found a weak, ragged one. The gunman had lost consciousness again, and would probably never regain it this time.

"Marshal, I would like to get Alice back to the hotel," Blackstreet said a little impatiently. "This has all been a terrible shock to her, just terrible."

Longarm pushed himself to his feet. "You're right, Sir Harry. Let's go."

But as they left, he glanced back one more time at the gutshot man and frowned.

As Longarm expected, Sir Harry was staying in one of Denver's best hotels. Not only that, but the visiting Englishman had the best suite in the house, complete with a sitting room and two bedrooms. That surprised Longarm a little, but he supposed it was for appearance's sake. It wouldn't look good if an uncle and niece were sharing one bedroom.

"I believe I'll lie down for a bit," Alice said when the three of them entered the suite's sitting room. She took off her hat and placed it on a side table, and as she did so, Longarm noticed that her hands were still trembling slightly.

"Of course, my dear," Sir Harry said. Solicitously, he unfastened the top button of her dress and fanned the material back and forth on her exposed throat for a moment. "You need some rest after that ordeal."

Alice gave him a weak smile and said, "Thank you, Uncle." She turned and went to the door of one of the bedrooms, disappearing inside and closing it firmly behind her.

"Poor girl," Sir Harry said. "No matter how much we men enjoy the heat of combat, we sometimes forget just what fragile flowers the ladies are."

"I've never particularly enjoyed being shot at," Longarm said honestly. "So I don't reckon I blame Miss Alice for being a mite spooked."

"Now, now, no false modesty, Marshal. I witnessed for myself your expertise with a weapon and your coolness

17

under fire, remember? Gad, I would have liked to have had a hundred like you in my brigade in the Crimea! Tell me, sir, have you ever served under arms?"

"Well, I fought in the Late Unpleasantness over here, what some folks call the War Between the States. But don't ask me which side I was on, because I sort of disremember, and at this late date, it ain't important anyway."

Blackstreet chuckled. "Indeed. What matters is that I'm certain you served with distinction."

"I made it out alive," Longarm said dryly. "That ain't something everybody can say."

Sir Harry turned toward a cabinet on one wall. "Would you care for a drink?"

It was a mite early in the day, Longarm thought, but then he gave a mental shrug. "Much obliged." As Sir Harry swung the cabinet doors open, revealing an array of liquor bottles that sparkled in the light from the gas chandelier, Longarm asked, "You wouldn't happen to have any Maryland rye in there, would you?"

"I'm afraid not. Some cognac perhaps?"

Longarm had always found that stuff a little fruity-tasting, but he didn't want to offend his host. He nodded and said, "Sure."

Sir Harry took the cork out of a decanter and poured the stuff into stemmed crystal glasses. He handed one to Longarm and lifted his own. "To the United States of America," he said. "A grand place!"

"I'll drink to that," Longarm agreed. Then, thinking that good manners called upon him to make a similar response, he said, "To the, uh, British Empire."

"May the sun never set on it," said Sir Harry. He drained the rest of the liquor in his glass, and Longarm followed suit. "Another?"

The cognac had gone down smooth, too smooth for it to be safe for Longarm to have another drink. He couldn't afford to get drunk while he was working. He set the empty glass on the side table next to Alice's pert little hat and shook his head. "No, thanks. I'll smoke a cheroot, though, if you don't mind."

Blackstreet laughed. "Not if you don't mind this foul-smelling old briar of mine." He took a pipe and a tobacco pouch from an inside pocket of his coat, then pointed with the stem of the pipe at an armchair. "Please, sit down, Marshal. Make yourself comfortable."

Both men settled in overstuffed armchairs and got their smokes going. When the cheroot was burning to Longarm's satisfaction, he said, "We got to talk about what happened at the museum, Sir Harry."

A petulant frown appeared on the Englishman's face, making him look more like a giant infant than ever. "I was hoping we could swap war stories."

"Maybe another time. Right now, I want to know why folks keep pointing guns at you."

Sir Harry shook his head. "I truly wish I knew. This trend toward encounters with the lawless has been the most distressing aspect of my visit to your country."

"You're certain the gents in Chicago and the ones on the train were the same bunch?"

"Indubitably. I recognized the voice of the man who spoke both times."

"What about their faces?"

"Well, I couldn't swear to that. They were masked, you see."

The reports Longarm had read hadn't mentioned that. "But you're sure—"

"I never forget a man's voice. Besides, the others on the train were built the same and dressed the same as the group that accosted us in Chicago. They were the same men."

Longarm wasn't completely convinced of that, but he was willing to accept Blackstreet's claim of recognizing the voice of the leader. It was possible that whoever was after him had recruited one bunch of crooks to jump him in Chicago and another to make the attempt on the train. Or maybe all the men had been the same ones. It didn't really matter, Longarm realized.

19

"And these fellas today weren't them?"

"Definitely not. The spokesman's voice was quite different, and some of these men were wearing, what would you call them, cowboy garments?"

"They were dressed cow, all right," Longarm agreed, "but a fella can change clothes in just a few minutes."

Blackstreet inclined his head in acknowledgment of Longarm's point. "True. I still feel that they were different men, however."

"We'll pass on that point for now," Longarm decided. "What did the men in Chicago say to you?"

Sir Harry puffed on his pipe for a moment and then said, "You know, that's a bit of an odd thing too. They threatened Alice and myself with guns and demanded that I hand it over. The spokesman didn't specify what *it* he was referring to."

"Your money?" Longarm suggested.

"That's what I took him to mean at the time, but now that I think about it, he could have been referring to something else. I have no idea what."

"And they got spooked and ran off before anything else was said?"

Sir Harry nodded solemnly. "That was the case, yes."

"And the men on the train? What did they say?"

"Only one of them spoke, and as I indicated earlier, I'm certain it was the same man who demanded *it* in Chicago. On this occasion, he said, and I quote, *You won't get away with it this time.* You see, that's another reason I'm sure he was the same man. His very words indicated a previous encounter. And again, there was a reference to *it.*"

Longarm's teeth clenched on the cheroot as he nodded. It sounded as if Blackstreet knew what he was talking about. But what had happened earlier today had sure muddied the waters.

"Those fellas today wanted *you,*" Longarm said. "That was supposed to be a kidnapping."

"Yes, but the ultimate goal could have been the same, could it not? Perhaps they intended to make me their pris-

20

oner so that they could torture me and force me to reveal the whereabouts of this mysterious object the other men were seeking. Perhaps they were a rival gang after the same thing."

"Well, they won't ever get their hands on it now," mused Longarm. "Whatever it is."

Sir Harry was right, he thought. Even though the method of today's incident had been different, the motivation could have been the same.

"You don't have any idea what those other gents were after?"

"None at all. I'm simply a businessman, combining business with pleasure as I make a tour of your American West on my way to inspect the mines owned by the British syndicate in which I'm a partner."

"Maybe the trouble has something to do with those mines," Longarm suggested, casting about for any reasonable explanation for the continued attacks on Sir Harry.

"I don't see how it could," Blackstreet replied with a frown. "We've had no problems at the mines that I'm aware of, no labor disputes or missing ore or anything of that sort. And the Indians in the area have long since stopped causing trouble."

Longarm sighed. "Well, like the old hymn says, farther along we'll know more about it. Until then, it's my job to keep you and your niece out of danger, Sir Harry."

"And I feel much better knowing that you're on the job, Marshal." Blackstreet set his pipe aside and put his hands on his knees, then heaved himself out of the chair to his feet. "I believe I shall follow Alice's example and lie down for a short time before the midday meal. I take it you'll be staying here?"

Longarm nodded. "Right here."

"Surely you don't think anything will happen here in the hotel?"

"You never know where trouble's coming from."

"I just don't want you to be uncomfortable."

21

Longarm smiled. "In the best suite in the house? I reckon I'll be comfortable enough, Sir Harry."

"Very well then. Help yourself to the liquor, if you care for another drink."

"Much obliged," said Longarm, even though he didn't intend to touch the cognac or anything else inside the liquor cabinet.

Blackstreet waddled into the second bedroom and closed the door behind him. Longarm cocked his right ankle on his left knee and smoked quietly for a while, finishing off the cheroot and snuffing out the butt in a sand-filled bucket sitting beside the cold fireplace. He wandered around the sitting room a little, taking in the luxurious furnishings. He had been in plenty of fancy places before, including this very hotel on several occasions. A place like this was nice for a change, but overall he preferred his rented room on the other side of Cherry Creek. He considered himself a simple man, with simple tastes.

A door latch clicked, and a soft voice said, "Marshal?"

Longarm turned and saw Alice Channing standing there in the doorway to her bedroom. She had opened more of the buttons on her dress, revealing a V-shaped wedge of the silken undergarment beneath it.

"Miss Channing," Longarm said. "What can I do for you?"

Alice smiled. "Well, to start with, you could come over here and kiss me."

Chapter 3

The suggestion took Longarm by surprise, but he thought he managed to keep his face fairly impassive. He shook his head slowly and said, "I don't think that would be a very good idea, Miss Alice."

"Call me Alice," she said. "And why wouldn't it be a good idea? You're a very handsome man, and I want to kiss you."

Longarm took a deep breath. "Well, for one thing, your uncle—"

"Is sound asleep," Alice interrupted. "Listen. Can't you hear him?" She gestured toward the closed door of the other bedroom.

Now that Longarm was paying attention, he could indeed hear the muffled rumble of snoring coming from behind the door. Sir Harry was sawing wood pretty good in there.

"Once he's asleep like that, an earthquake wouldn't disturb him," Alice went on. "So you don't have to worry about anything Uncle Harry might say or do. He'll never know about it."

Longarm was tempted, no two ways about it. Alice Channing was a mighty pretty young woman. But whether she was Blackstreet's mistress, as Longarm believed, or really his niece, it didn't matter. Longarm didn't have any business kissing her while he was working.

Her fingers lifted to the top button of her dress that was still fastened, and Longarm hoped sincerely that she wasn't planning on unbuttoning any more of them.

"Are you sure I can't entice you, Marshal?" she asked as she started to do just that. Deftly, her fingers flicked three more buttons open, and a shrug of her shoulders made the dress fall off them, revealing the slender straps of a chemise and a good deal of smooth, creamy skin.

Well, hell, he was only human, Longarm told himself.

A couple of strides brought him within reach of Alice, who tilted her face up, closed her eyes, and parted her lips expectantly as Longarm's hands extended toward her.

He caught hold of her dress, jerked it closed, and started buttoning it up.

"Oh!" Alice gasped as she realized she wasn't being kissed after all. Now that he was closer to her, Longarm could smell alcohol on her breath. She hadn't gone in the bedroom to lie down, he realized. What she'd really been after was a little nip to steady her nerves and work up her courage.

"Listen," he said quietly, "you're a fine-looking lady, Miss Alice, and I reckon I'm liable to regret this my whole blamed life, but if I was to kiss you now I'd be taking advantage of you, and I don't want to do that."

"But . . . but . . ."

"You just hush now," Longarm told her as he buttoned another button, all too aware of how the swells of her breasts brushed against the backs of his hands. "We won't say anything more about this. It'll be our secret."

"Damn it, if we're going to have a secret, I'd rather it was that you'd just given me a good, hard—"

"None of that," Longarm cut in firmly. He had the buttons fastened almost all the way up to her neck now. He decided that was good enough, and laid his hands on her shoulders to turn her around. "You run along—"

She jerked free of his grip, whirled around, and threw

24

her arms around his neck. Short of walloping her, which he didn't want to do, there was no way Longarm could stop her from pressing her body against his and hungrily seeking his mouth with her lips.

She tasted of booze too, or maybe it was just one of those "ladies' tonics" that were mostly alcohol. Other than that she was a damned good kisser. Her lips were open, and her tongue slid daringly into his mouth. Her hips pressed forward, grinding her stomach against his groin. In spite of his resolve not to allow it to happen, Longarm's manhood responded in the usual fashion, quickly stiffening into a long, thick rod that Alice had to feel prodding against her belly.

She finally took her lips away from his and whispered, "See, I told you you'd enjoy it."

"That ain't the point." Longarm took hold of her arms and as gently as possible disengaged them from around his neck. He took a step back, but held her where she was so there would be some distance separating them. "It ain't a good idea for the two of us to be fooling around. The only reason I'm here is because somebody keeps threatening you and your uncle. I got to pay attention to that and nothing else."

She glared at him and tried to pull her arms loose from his hands, but this time he was ready for her and his grip was too strong. "You don't have to be so . . . so bloody noble about it!" she snapped. "It wouldn't hurt anything for you and me to have a bit of fun."

"Maybe not, but I don't plan on taking that chance." Longarm finally let go of her and stepped back again. "You should go on back in your room, Miss Alice, and this time you really ought to lie down for a while."

She drew herself up and crossed her arms in front of her, the picture of offended dignity. Haughtily, she asked, "Whatever do you mean by that?"

"I mean you better not take any more nips from whatever you've been drinking," Longarm said bluntly. "You've had enough."

Her eyes glittered icily as she said, "I have no idea what you're talking about." She swayed a little to the side as she spoke.

"Fine." Longarm took his watch from his vest pocket and flipped it open to check the time. "I imagine we'll be going down to lunch in an hour or so. That'll give you time to rest a spell."

"You're a fool, a bloody damned fool."

"Yes, ma'am, I expect you're right," Longarm said as he closed his watch and put it away.

She was still glaring at him as she turned unsteadily toward the door, opened it, and went back into the bedroom. Longarm hoped she wouldn't slam the door behind her, regardless of what she had said about how difficult it was to disturb Sir Harry once he was asleep. Longarm didn't want to take a chance on that.

Alice didn't close the door at all. Instead she left it wide open as she went over to the bed. She must have been unbuttoning the dress again as she went, because she peeled it off in a hurry and tossed it aside, leaving her clad only in a chemise and a long slip. With her back still toward the door, she pushed the slip down over her hips and stepped out of it, then grasped the bottom of the chemise and peeled it up and over her head. She tossed it aside, too.

Then, naked except for a pair of stockings that came up over her calves, she looked back over her shoulder and smiled triumphantly at Longarm. He sighed, reached into the room to grasp the doorknob, and quietly pulled the door closed.

He'd been right about one thing, he told himself.

Miss Alice Channing's bare backside was every bit as good as the one on that statue in the museum. Better, even, right down to the dimple in the middle of her left cheek.

Alice was quiet and a bit pale during the lunch she shared with Longarm and Sir Harry in the hotel dining room. Longarm didn't know if she had taken his advice about not drinking anymore. But she didn't make any reference to what had happened between them—or what *hadn't* happened—and he was glad of that.

"I was planning to spend more time in your fair city," Sir Harry said as he attacked with vigor a plate filled with fried steak and potatoes, "but I've begun to wonder if under the circumstances it might be best to travel on to Nevada as quickly as possible."

Longarm mulled that over for a moment, then said, "It'd be a shame if you didn't get to do as much sight-seeing as you wanted to, Sir Harry, but I reckon you're right. The sooner you get your business done, the better."

"My thoughts exactly. I'm told that the syndicate's mines are near a settlement known as Virginia City. Are you familiar with it, Marshal Long?"

"Been there a time or three," Longarm said. To tell the truth, his job had taken him to Virginia City quite a few times. He was very familiar with the settlement nestled in the Nevada mountains near the world-famous Comstock Lode.

"Alice and I can travel there by train, can we not?"

Longarm nodded. "Sure. You'll just have to go back up to Cheyenne on the Denver & Rio Grande, then connect with the Union Pacific up there. It'll take us almost due west to Salt Lake City, in Utah, and then across to Virginia City in Nevada."

"Us?" Sir Harry repeated with a slight smile.

"I plan on going with you." Longarm glanced at Alice. He might be letting himself in for some extra trouble by keeping himself in close proximity to her, but after that corpse-and-cartridge session at the museum this morning, he didn't think it would be a good idea to let her and Sir Harry go on to Nevada by themselves.

"Then, if I understand correctly, your jurisdiction extends as far as Virginia City?" asked Blackstreet.

"I'm a federal lawman," Longarm explained. "My jurisdiction ends at the United States borders, and that's all."

Sir Harry picked up the big glass of lemonade he had ordered with the meal. "Then I see I did the right thing by wiring the British embassy in Washington and asking that they request help from your government."

"Yes, sir, as long as my boss goes along with it, and I'm sure he will."

Longarm knew he would have to talk to Billy Vail before he left Denver with Sir Harry and Alice, though, so after they were finished with the meal, he stopped by the desk in the hotel lobby and asked the clerk to send somebody to the Federal Building with a message. Longarm scribbled a few words on a piece of paper that the clerk provided, using a pencil that also came from the clerk, then folded the paper and gave it to the bellboy who answered the clerk's summons. "Take that to Chief Marshal Vail's office in the Federal Building," Longarm told the boy. "If Marshal Vail ain't there, you can give it to the pasty-faced little gent who'll be in the outer office." Henry hardly ever left his post, preferring to eat lunch at his desk every day.

Sir Harry and Alice were waiting for him. He walked back up to the suite with them. Alice went to her room again, leaving Longarm and Sir Harry to pass the time in the sitting room. Sir Harry got his story-swapping wish, although Longarm chose not to talk about the war and spun a few yarns instead about some of the cases he'd worked on as a marshal. Sir Harry seemed to enjoy them just as well.

After about an hour, a knock sounded on the door. Longarm stood up to answer it. He put his hand on the butt of his Colt as he called, "Who's out there?" Then he stepped quickly to one side in case anybody tried to blast through the door with a shotgun or something like that.

"It's just me and Willie, Longarm," came the reply. "Don't get your fur in an uproar."

Longarm grinned and took his hand off his gun. He had locked the door when he and Sir Harry and Alice returned to the room. Now he twisted the key in the lock and opened the door.

A couple of middle-aged, competent-looking men in suits and dark Stetsons stepped into the room. Longarm gave them a friendly nod and closed the door behind them. Blackstreet was regarding the newcomers curiously, so Longarm said, "Sir Harry, these are a couple of my fellow deputy marshals. Scott, Willie, meet Sir Harry Blackstreet."

Sir Harry lumbered to his feet and shook hands with both of the men. Turning to Longarm, he said, "So you've called in reinforcements, eh, Marshal?"

"I've got to go back and talk to my boss, and while I'm at it I'll arrange for our train tickets. Scott and Willie will keep an eye on you while I'm gone."

"Are you certain that's a good idea?" Sir Harry asked with a slight frown.

"These two have brought in plenty of bad hombres. They can take care of themselves, and you and Miss Alice."

"Very well, Marshal Long, I shall trust in your good judgment."

Longarm left them there, after making sure the door was locked behind him, and walked quickly down the street to the Federal Building. Henry waved him on through, directly into Billy Vail's office.

"I suppose Scott and Willie got to the hotel all right," Vail said by way of greeting.

"I left 'em in Sir Harry's suite."

Vail grunted and picked up a piece of paper from his desk. "I got this report from the Denver police. Seems that there was some sort of dustup at the art museum this morning. Five men ended up dead, and a guard was wounded."

"Wouldn't think something like that would happen at a museum, would you?" Longarm asked as he sat down in the red leather chair.

"Damn it, Custis!" Vail exploded. "What in blazes happened?"

"The same thing that happened in Chicago and on the train here," Longarm replied grimly. "Some gents with guns came after Sir Harry. Only this time they tried to kidnap him, instead of just holding him up." Longarm didn't go into the possibility that the gunmen in all three cases might have been after some mysterious object that Sir Harry claimed was unknown to him.

"It looks mighty bad that this could happen right here in Denver," Vail said.

Longarm shrugged. "It would have been worse if those gunnies had gotten away with it, I reckon."

"True enough," admitted Vail. "I guess that note you sent me means you intend to go on to Nevada with Blackstreet and his niece."

Longarm didn't mention being convinced that Alice wasn't Sir Harry's niece either, and he certainly didn't say anything about the kiss they'd shared or the little exhibition of flesh she had put on for him. He just said, "Under the circumstances, I think it'd be a good idea."

"I do too," Vail said. "In fact, if you hadn't volunteered, I'd have given you the job anyway. Get your expense money and travel vouchers from Henry on the way out. I already had him type up the vouchers."

Longarm rose. "I don't know how long I'll be gone. Sir Harry wants to head on to Virginia City right away."

"The sooner he's out of Denver, the better," Vail muttered. "Just you keep a close eye on him, Custis. The State Department'll give Justice hell if we let him get himself killed."

"May the sun never set on the British Empire," Longarm said under his breath.

"What?" Vail snapped.

But Longarm was already gone, swinging the office door shut behind him.

There was a train leaving at five that afternoon for Cheyenne. Longarm stopped at the depot and picked up tickets for himself, Sir Harry Blackstreet, and Miss Alice Channing. They would get into Cheyenne in the evening and would have to spend the night there. A Union Pacific westbound would be leaving sometime the next day, though Longarm didn't know exactly when.

With Scott and Willie at the hotel watching out for Sir

Harry and Alice, Longarm took the time to go by his rented room and throw a few things in his carpetbag. He was in the habit of traveling light, but he still liked to have a clean shirt handy just in case he needed it—not to mention a couple of boxes of .44 cartridges. He left his McClellan saddle, not expecting that he would have any need of it, but hesitated over his Winchester. Carrying a rifle on the train was a pain in the rear end, but in his line of work you never knew when you might need one. He finally tucked the weapon under his arm and took it with him.

"Going bear hunting?" Scott asked when he let Longarm back into the hotel room. He grinned.

"Might get me a grizzly on the way back," Longarm said with an answering grin. "Anything happen while I was gone?"

"Sir Harry told us all about England," Willie said.

"We had a wonderful time," Blackstreet said. "These associates of yours are quite the raconteurs."

Longarm wasn't exactly sure what that meant, and from the looks on their faces, neither were Willie and Scott, but Sir Harry obviously meant it as a compliment. Scott said, "Much obliged, Sir Harry," then turned to Longarm and asked, "You need us to stick around for a while?"

Longarm shook his head. "Nope. You boys can go on home." He followed them into the hall, pulled the door mostly shut behind him, and added in a quiet voice, "We'll be heading down to the train station a little before five. Keep an eye on our backtrail, will you?"

The two deputies nodded in understanding. Longarm had no reason to be suspicious of Sir Harry—just the opposite, in fact—but it never hurt to hedge your bets. Unknown to anyone except Longarm, Scott and Willie would be watching in case anyone tried to follow the small party to the depot.

Longarm went back into the suite and looked around. "Where's Miss Alice?" he asked.

"Resting again," Sir Harry replied. "I'm afraid this morning's adventure affected her more than she would like to

31

admit. She's not accustomed to bullets flying around her."

"It ain't an easy thing to get used to."

Sir Harry rubbed his hands together. "Well, sir, I take it we shall be departing soon from Denver?"

"We're on the five o'clock train to Cheyenne. We'll stay there tonight and catch the westbound tomorrow."

"Excellent. How many days will it take us to reach Virginia City?"

"A couple. There are a lot of high mountain passes between here and there. In country like that, with steep grades, a train can't make very good time."

"It doesn't matter," Blackstreet said with a wave of his hand. "Our mining superintendent isn't expecting me at any particular time. He was just told that I would be making an inspection tour sometime this month."

Longarm found himself wondering about that. Sir Harry had claimed that the mines were in good shape, lucrative enterprises with no real trouble hanging over them. But maybe there was something he and his partners in the syndicate didn't know. Maybe somebody connected with the mines had a good reason not to want Sir Harry to make that inspection. One way to stop him would be to have him killed in a phony robbery or kidnapping. That would delay any inspection of the mines for months, at the very least.

It was a thought anyway. Longarm couldn't afford to close his mind to any possibility right now.

Alice still looked wan when she emerged from her room later. Sir Harry told her to pack her bags, and when she had done that, Longarm carried them into the sitting room for her. When he passed her, he didn't smell any liquor on her breath. Either she'd gotten better at hiding it, or she hadn't had a drink this afternoon.

When he was at the train station earlier, he had made arrangements for a carriage to call at the hotel a little before five. Bellboys loaded the baggage, and Longarm sat up front with the driver, the Winchester across his lap, as the carriage rolled down to the station. Everything went smoothly. On the train, Longarm got Sir Harry and Alice settled in their seats—not that easy a chore considering Sir Harry's bulk—then stepped out onto the platform at the rear of the car for a last glance around. The deputy called Scott was idling near the board where the train schedule was chalked. He gave Longarm a high sign to indicate that no one had followed them. Longarm went back into the car and sat down across from Sir Harry and Alice.

"Next stop, Cheyenne, I reckon," he said, and a few minutes later, with the grinding of steel drivers on the rails and the shrill blast of the whistle from the locomotive, the train rolled out of the station heading north.

Chapter 4

The sun setting over the Front Range to the west was a magnificent sight, one that Longarm never got tired of seeing. Sir Harry and Alice were seated on the left-hand side of the aisle, so they had an even better view of the scenery. "This is a beautiful country you have here, Marshal," Sir Harry told Longarm.

"Much obliged. I'm right fond of it too."

The trip from Denver to Cheyenne took a little over three hours. Dusk had settled down over the Wyoming town as the train pulled into the station. Longarm stepped out onto the lantern-lit platform first, his keen eyes scanning it for any sign of possible trouble. Quite a few people were coming and going, but none of them looked particularly threatening. He turned his head and nodded to Sir Harry and Alice, who were waiting patiently for him to give them the go-ahead.

They moved onto the platform while Longarm signaled for a porter to unload their baggage. Longarm asked the man, "Is the Cattleman's Hotel still right down the street?"

"That's right, mister. That where you're goin'?"

The Cattleman's was one of the best hotels in Cheyenne, and it was close to the train station. Those two qualities had made Longarm choose it for tonight's stopover. He nodded to the porter and said, "Have our bags brought down there, would you, old son?"

The porter deftly snagged out of midair the coin that Longarm flipped to him and nodded, grinning. "Sure thing, mister."

Longarm turned to Sir Harry and Alice. "We'll go straight to the hotel," he told them. "The dining room there is good, so we can get some dinner without having to leave."

"Whatever you say, Marshal. We are in your hands," Sir Harry said.

Longarm ushered them toward the double doors that led from the station platform into the depot itself. As he did so, one of the other disembarking passengers caught his eye. The man was tall and so thin that his clothes hung on him like a scarecrow's rags. He wasn't wearing a hat, so his long, tangled thatch of sandy hair was plainly visible. He sported a narrow mustache and a small goatee. A silk cloak was fastened around his neck and draped over his shoulders. That was something you didn't see every day, thought Longarm. The rest of the fella's clothes were rather shabby, but a cloak like that was expensive. He sure didn't look like someone who would typically be found in the train station at Cheyenne, Wyoming.

But he didn't look dangerous either, and he didn't even glance in the direction of Longarm, Blackstreet, and Alice as he moved instead to the end of the platform and went down the steps there. Obviously, he planned to go around the depot, rather than through the lobby. Longarm kept an eye on the man until he'd disappeared around the corner of the building, then turned his attention back to his two charges. "Our bags will be delivered to the hotel," he told them. "We'll sign in, then go straight to the dining room."

"A capital idea," agreed Sir Harry. "It's been too long since that midday meal in Denver."

Of course, that wasn't the last time Sir Harry had eaten, Longarm reflected. The Englishman had polished off several apples and a couple of sandwiches he'd bought from a boy who was selling them on the train. Clearly, Sir Harry had quite an appetite.

Cheyenne was a cow town, the chief supply point for the scores of ranches to the north and west. Denver prided itself on being a more cosmopolitan city, but there were few frills to Cheyenne. Most of the streets were unpaved, and the traffic they carried consisted mainly of cowboys on horseback, ranch wagons, and buckboards. There were cavalry troopers in evidence as well, and even a few tame Indians. Every block boasted at least two saloons or gambling halls or dance halls. Due to the warm weather, doors were open, allowing the tinny strains of player piano music to float out into the evening. Sir Harry took it all in avidly and finally exclaimed, "I say! It's like something out of one of your American dime novels."

Longarm was a little surprised that an English nobleman and financier was familiar with the lurid yarns that were published in cheap, yellow-backed editions, but he supposed there was no telling what folks might read. Alice looked less interested in the slices of Western life around her.

It took only a few minutes to walk to the Cattleman's Hotel from the train station. The three-story building, made of native stone quarried in the Laramie Mountains to the west, was an impressive structure. Given the season, Longarm figured he and his companions would be able to get rooms. Earlier in the year, during the spring roundup time, the place would have been full of ranchers and cattle buyers.

They went inside, and Longarm spoke to the desk clerk, a man with slicked-down hair parted in the middle of his head. He was eager to please, especially when he saw Longarm's badge. "Yes, sir, Marshal, we can put you up. Got a couple of adjoinin' rooms and one right across the hall."

"That'll do," Longarm said. Sir Harry and Alice could take the adjoining rooms. Ideally, they would drop the pose as uncle and niece and go ahead and share a room, so that Longarm could take the one adjoining, but he didn't feel that he could suggest that. If his suspicions about their relationship were wrong, it would be improper as hell to recommend such an arrangement. He would just have to stay across the hall and trust to the fact that he could be a mighty light sleeper when he needed to be.

After telling the clerk to have their bags taken up to the rooms when they arrived from the depot, Longarm led Sir Harry and Alice into the dining room, which was still busy despite the fairly late hour. They sat at a round table in a corner that was partially screened from the rest of the room by a couple of potted plants. After about a minute, a slightly plump, brunette waitress in a gingham dress and a white apron came up to the table and greeted the three of them with a smile. "What can I get you folks this evening?" she asked.

"I assume you sell steaks?" Sir Harry asked before Longarm could say anything.

"Why, yes, sir, we sure do. The best in the whole state of Wyoming."

With a smile, Sir Harry leaned back in his chair, laced his hands together over his ample belly, and said, "Bring me the largest, thickest steak you have, cooked medium-rare, if you please. I would also like boiled potatoes, some sort of vegetable if you have it, and an ample amount of bread. Bring a pot of coffee with that. And what sort of sweets do you have?"

"Apple pie and peach cobbler," the waitress responded.

"I'll have one of each."

"Yes, sir." She looked at Longarm and Alice. "And for you folks?"

"A bowl of soup, please," Alice requested quietly.

"We've got a fresh pot of son-of-a-bitch stew. Is that all right?"

Longarm chuckled at the look on Alice's face. "It's better than it sounds," he assured her.

37

Alice nodded and said to the waitress, "That will be fine, thank you."

The brunette looked at Longarm, and he saw the frank interest in her eyes as she took in his rugged features and rangy form. "What about you, sir? What would you like?" she asked.

Longarm couldn't help but wonder if she meant something else by that question. He said, "I'll have what Sir Harry's having, but make my steak well done. And I reckon I'll stick with the peach cobbler and pass on the apple pie this time."

"Yes, sir. I'll tell the cook and be right back with your coffee."

Longarm watched her walk away, admiring the sway of her backside as she did so. It was a subtle, sensuous movement, not a blatant one, and Longarm found himself wondering what it would feel like to have the pillowy cushions of that rump snuggled up against him.

"That woman flirted shamelessly with you!" Alice hissed.

"Did she?" Longarm said. "I didn't notice."

Sir Harry let out a booming laugh that drew some attention from the other diners. Longarm wished he wouldn't do that, but he figured it would be pretty difficult to get a man like Sir Harry to tone down any of his actions. The Englishman seemed to enjoy acting flamboyantly.

"You should open your eyes, Marshal," advised Blackstreet. "One never knows what treasures one might find right under one's nose."

"I reckon one don't," Longarm agreed.

The bold-eyed waitress came back to the table a few minutes later carrying a coffeepot with a leather holder. She had a tray with three cups on it in her other hand. She served them smoothly and efficiently, filling the cups with coffee and placing one in front of each of them, even Alice, who hadn't specifically asked for coffee. "I'll be back with a pitcher of cream," the waitress said.

Longarm didn't need cream; he drank his Arbuckle's

black, and he could tell by the aroma rising from the cup along with wisps of steam that was the brew the hotel used in its kitchen. He just nodded his thanks to the waitress, though, and got a dazzling smile in return.

From the corner of his eye, he saw the disapproving frown on Alice's face. She was getting angry, thought Longarm. Not only had he turned down her advances earlier in the day, but now she was being forced to sit here and watch another woman flirting with him. He hoped that before the evening was over, Alice and the waitress wouldn't wind up rolling around on the floor, pulling each other's hair and trying to scratch each other's eyes out. He didn't feel much like refereeing such a battle.

Perhaps luckily, some cowboys at another table began demanding more service, so the pretty brunette waitress was kept busy and didn't have time to do anything other than deliver the food to Longarm and his two companions. Sir Harry dug in with his usual gusto, and Longarm followed suit. Alice just picked at her bowl of son-of-a-bitch stew, making faces at some of the things she found in it.

Sir Harry had no trouble polishing off the massive steak he was brought, nor the potatoes and turnip greens and big hunks of cornbread that came with it. Longarm decided he didn't ever want to get into an eating contest with the Englishman. He enjoyed his own meal, especially the peach cobbler with its flaky crust dusted with sugar.

When they were finished, Sir Harry pushed his empty plates away and sighed contentedly. "A meal fit for a king—or a cattle baron. Bravo, Marshal."

Longarm shook his head. "I didn't cook it."

"No, but you selected this establishment, and in doing so you displayed admirable taste. You'll come with us back up to our rooms, so that we can share a smoke and perhaps a snifter of brandy before retiring?"

"Sure." Longarm didn't intend to say good night to Sir Harry and Alice until they were ready to turn in.

As they left the dining room, the brunette waitress managed to be near the door. She smiled at Longarm and said, "You come on back any time, hear?"

Longarm tugged on the brim of his Stetson and nodded pleasantly. "Much obliged, ma'am."

When they reached the lobby, Alice muttered under her breath, "I still think it's shameful the way that hussy was throwing herself at you, Marshal."

At least she didn't peel all her duds off right in the middle of the dining room, thought Longarm. That right there made her more discreet than some young ladies he could mention.

But he kept those thoughts to himself and said, "Oh, I don't reckon she meant anything by it."

He knew better, however. The waitress had been interested in him, and to tell the truth, he had found her pretty attractive too. But he didn't expect anything would come of it. After all, he and his companions were only going to be in Cheyenne one night.

A word to the desk clerk was enough to send a boy scurrying over to one of the saloons to bring back a bottle of brandy. Longarm drew the kid aside and slipped him some extra money to buy a bottle of Maryland rye too. He would put it in his carpetbag for the rest of the journey. He would have bought some in Denver and bought it with him, he thought, if he hadn't been in such a hurry to pack.

Within a short time, the three of them were comfortably ensconced in Sir Harry's room. Longarm lit a cheroot, while the Englishman fired up his pipe. They took the two armchairs, while Alice made herself comfortable on a small divan, drawing her legs up and tucking them underneath her. Longarm thought that made her look even younger than she was, and mighty cute. She thumbed through a copy of *Harper's Magazine* she had brought up with her from the lobby, while Longarm and Sir Harry discussed mining. Longarm had been to the Comstock Lode several times, and he answered Blackstreet's questions about the area and the various mining operations there as best he could.

Finally, Alice began to yawn. She put the magazine

aside, stood up, and stretched. That made her breasts press hard against the bosom of her dress, Longarm noticed. She said, "I believe I shall retire for the evening."

"A splendid idea," Sir Harry agreed. "When does the westbound train depart tomorrow, Marshal?"

Longarm had checked the schedule at the depot. "Nine-forty-five in the morning," he said.

"Then we won't have to rise too terribly early. We should even have time for a leisurely breakfast."

Longarm nodded. He found himself wondering if the same waitress would be working in the dining room in the morning. Probably not, he decided, since she had been on duty fairly late this evening.

Alice went into the adjoining room and closed the door. Longarm didn't expect to see her again until the next morning. She surprised him, however, by reappearing a few minutes later. She had taken off her traveling outfit and replaced it with a silk dressing gown. She came over to the chair where Sir Harry was sitting and said, "Good night, Uncle." She leaned over to plant a kiss on his bald head.

As she did so, the dressing gown parted slightly, and from where he was sitting, Longarm had a good view of her breasts. He could see a lot of them, even parts of both nipples, dark brown against the creamy flesh surrounding them, and he figured Alice was naked under the gown.

Sir Harry seemed not to notice. He gave her a perfunctory pat on the shoulder and said, "Sleep well, my dear."

Maybe he had been wrong, Longarm thought, and Sir Harry and Alice really were uncle and niece. Or if she was his mistress, maybe Blackstreet was one of those gents who didn't mind when his woman flaunted herself in front of other men. At any rate, Longarm forced his eyes away from Alice's breasts, but not quickly enough. He caught the flicker of triumph in her eyes as she straightened and said, "Good night, Marshal."

He nodded and said, "Good night, ma'am. Like your uncle said, sleep well."

"I'm certain that I shall." She turned and walked back

into the adjoining room. The door clicked shut behind her.

Sir Harry puffed on his pipe for a moment longer, then said, "I suppose I should call it a night as well. Are you anticipating any trouble, Marshal?"

"We didn't sneak out of Denver," Longarm said. "If somebody was keeping an eye on us, they know where we are. I don't expect anybody would try anything in a hotel like this . . . but I didn't think anybody would try to jump you at an art museum either."

"A point well taken. I assume you shall be in the room across the hall."

"Unless I decide to find a chair and spend the night sitting up in the hall."

Sir Harry shook his head. "I wouldn't want you to be so sorely inconvenienced, Marshal. I'm sure Alice and I shall be fine. But just in case . . ." He reached inside his coat and produced a small revolver. "I *am* armed."

"If anybody busts in here, don't hesitate to use it," Longarm advised him.

"Never doubt that I shall."

"Be sure and lock the door behind me."

"Of course."

Satisfied that he had taken as many precautions as he could, Longarm said good night to Sir Harry and went across the hall to his own room, taking the bottle of rye with him. The door was locked. He unlocked it and stepped inside, leaving the door open until he had found the lamp on the little bedside table and lit it with a lucifer he snapped into life on an iron-hard thumbnail. His carpetbag and his Winchester were lying on the bed. He checked the bag and found that no one had disturbed its contents. The rifle was unloaded, just the way he had left it. He leaned it in a corner of the room and started to undress.

He was down to the bottom half of his long underwear—he didn't wear the top half in weather as warm as this—when a soft knock sounded on the door. He hadn't heard any footsteps in the hall outside the room, so whoever was out there knew how to move quietly. Nor had he heard either of the doors across the hall open, and he had been listening for such sounds. He was confident that Sir Harry and Alice were still secure behind the locked doors of their rooms.

Longarm wasn't expecting anyone, so he snagged the Colt from the holster attached to the shell belt he had hung over one of the bedposts. Once he had his fingers wrapped around the smooth walnut grips of the gun, he bent over and blew out the lamp. The knock sounded again on the door.

Longarm waited a few more seconds, letting his eyes adjust to the darkness inside the room. If this was trouble, he wanted any advantage he could get. He cat-footed closer to the door and listened.

The knock came yet again, and this time it was accompanied by a whispered voice. "Marshal Long? Are you in there?"

Longarm let out the breath he had been holding without even being aware of it. He recognized the voice. It belonged to the pretty brunette waitress from the dining room.

That didn't mean he relaxed completely. Chances were, the woman had come up there because she was feeling randy, but he couldn't be sure of that. Someone who was after Sir Harry might have bribed the waitress to lure Longarm out of his room, or she might have been forced to knock on his door at gunpoint. Longarm reached down, turned the key in the lock as soundlessly as possible, then grasped the knob and twisted it. He jerked the door open and quickly stepped back and to the side.

"Oh!" the woman gasped.

She was alone, Longarm saw instantly. She had taken off the apron but still wore the gingham dress. He moved forward enough to cast a glance both ways along the hall. It was empty except for the waitress.

"My Lord, Marshal, do you greet all your visitors like that, wearing just your underwear and waving a gun around? I don't really mind, but you gave me sort of a start."

"Sorry," Longarm said. He lowered the Colt, but didn't put it away. He didn't have any place to put it. He damned sure wasn't going to tuck it into the waistband of his underwear and risk shooting himself in the balls. He went on. "What can I do for you?"

The woman looked a little embarrassed. She probably didn't do this sort of thing too often. "Well, since you're a guest here, I just thought I ought to check and make sure you're comfortable. What with you being a lawman and all."

"The room's just fine," Longarm said.

"Is there . . . anything I can get you? Anything at all?"

Longarm smiled, well aware that he was being a bit of a scoundrel for teasing her this way. "Can't think of a thing I need," he told her.

"Oh. Well . . . maybe I'd better check your room just in case there's something the maid forgot when she fixed it up."

Longarm stepped back. "Sure, come on in."

He turned his back to her to close the door behind her, thinking that this would be a good test of whether she really wanted to go through with this. If she didn't, she would probably object to him closing the door.

When he turned back to her, he saw that she had made up her mind, all right. She must have gone somewhere and taken off every stitch of clothes under the gingham dress, because she was pulling it over her head already and was naked as a jaybird underneath it.

Chapter 5

The woman might have been carrying some extra pounds on her in some folks' opinion, but to Longarm she looked damned fine as he got a match from the pocket of his vest lying on a chair and relit the lamp. Her breasts were large and firm and rode fairly high on her chest. Their nipples were pink, not much darker than the rest of her skin, and at least two inches in diameter. The belly underneath the breasts was slightly rounded and sloped down smoothly to her abdomen. Her thighs were strong, not flabby, and the triangle of hair where they joined was dark and thick. The hair on her head was equally dark and fell in waves to her shoulders as she pulled some pins from it and freed it from the bun in which she had worn it while she was working. She kicked her shoes off and stood before Longarm totally nude.

As his eyes moved leisurely over her and took in all the wonders of her lush body, she started blushing. Longarm thought that made her even prettier. "I'm not a . . . a soiled dove," she said. "I didn't come up here looking for money."

"I knew that," Longarm told her, and meant it.

"I'm not a loose woman either. It's just that it's been a while since I've seen a man like you, Marshal." She glanced down at his groin, where his shaft was rapidly hardening inside his underwear. As her eyes widened slightly, she breathed, "I don't know that I've *ever* seen a man like you."

"I'll only be in Cheyenne tonight," Longarm told her as he came closer to her.

"I figured as much. That's why I decided I couldn't afford to wait."

Longarm smiled as he reached past her to replace the Colt in its holster. Her left breast brushed against his arm as he did so. "I admire a woman who knows what she wants," he told her.

"Well, I surely do know what I want," she said breathlessly, and then she came into his arms, lifting her face so that his mouth could come down hard on hers.

The kiss was urgent. Their lips parted and their tongues came together, darting and flickering back and forth as they explored each other's mouth. Longarm's arms went around her and drew her to him so that her breasts flattened against his chest. He slid his hands down the smooth skin of her back to the swell of her ample hips. His organ was rockhard by now and pressing against the softness of her belly.

She put her arms around him and moved her hands under the waistband of the underwear, cupping his buttocks as he was cupping hers. After a few moments of grinding her pelvis against his, she started tugging the underwear down. She broke the kiss and moved her head down to his chest, kissing the thick mat of dark brown hair that lay across it. As she lowered the underwear, his shaft sprang free, the head of it bobbing up and down slightly. Her lips were on his belly by then, and his underwear was down around his knees. She gave it a last push that sent it falling around his ankles, then wrapped both hands around his manhood and studied it avidly from a distance of a couple of inches. Her tongue darted out and licked over her lips in a promise of delights to come.

She fulfilled that promise a second later by leaning forward, opening her lips, and taking the head of his organ into her mouth. Her tongue swirled around it, wetting the rigid male flesh thoroughly as she sucked on it. She kept one hand on the thick shaft and dropped the other to his balls, gently cupping the sac and rolling the heavy orbs back and forth.

Longarm withstood that exquisite torment as long as he could, then, knowing that he would soon be spending his climax in her mouth if she didn't stop, caught hold of her shoulders and pulled her up from her kneeling position in front of him. She was breathless and heavy-lidded with lust. He cupped her chin and brushed another·kiss across her lips, then lowered his head to her left breast. The very center of the nipple had hardened into a little pink bud. He tapped it with his tongue, then closed his lips around it and sucked gently. The woman put her hands on his head and held it there, sighing as his lips and tongue caressed her.

After a while he moved his attention to her other breast. While he licked and sucked that nipple, he moved her toward the bed, and when the back of her legs hit the edge of the mattress, she lowered herself and lay back. Longarm went to his knees beside the bed as she opened her thighs, revealing the wet, pink folds of her femininity. Longarm spread the lips with the finger of his left hand, then ran the index finger of his right hand down the moist slit. The woman's hips worked involuntarily, and her core was so wet that his finger slipped easily into her. He added another finger to the first one and worked them back and forth, soaking them in her juices before leaning forward and replacing them with his tongue.

That had her hips bouncing hard on the mattress in a matter of seconds. Her breathing grew more rapid, and she let out a little moan. Longarm delved as deep as he could, at the same time using his thumb to rub the little nubbin of flesh at the top of her slit. Her legs went around his head and her thighs clamped against his ears. As always when he had brought a woman to the brink of culmination like this, he wondered if a fella could suffocate in this position. But that was a risk he had always been willing to run.

The woman stiffened, her torso coming up off the bed, then fell back and sighed a long, satisfied sigh. Her legs sagged open again, and Longarm lifted himself to his feet. The long, thick shaft still jutted out proudly and urgently from his groin. The woman's eyes were closed, but she opened them and smiled at the sight of what was still awaiting her. She scooted into the center of the bed and spread her legs wide in invitation.

Longarm moved over her, reveling in the softness of her thighs as he positioned his hips between them and brought the head of his pole to her opening. With a surge, he drove into her, sheathing himself almost fully. The woman gasped as he hitched his hips up to bury the last inch or so within her.

"Oh, my God," she moaned. "I've never felt anything like . . . that's the biggest I've ever . . . oh . . ."

Longarm launched into the timeless rhythm, his shaft moving smoothly in and out of her. In a matter of moments, both of them were covered in fine beads of sweat, and where they were joined together was drenched with moisture of another sort. What had come before had been wonderful, but now Longarm felt the urgent need for release building up inside him. His pace increased, growing both harder and faster. The woman's arms went around him, clasping him to her, and her ankles locked together above his buttocks to give herself some leverage as she met each of his thrusts with one of her own. Longarm kissed her again, filling her mouth with his tongue as he had filled her femininity with his manhood.

Then, with a shudder, he planted himself as deeply inside her as he could and felt his climax overtake him in a series of thunderous explosions. His seed boiled up from his balls and through his shaft, emptying itself in spurt after white-hot spurt. The woman might have screamed in ecstasy if Longarm's mouth had not been pressed so tightly to hers. She bucked and heaved under him, caught up in a culmination every bit as intense and passionate as his.

When the spasms coursing through them finally began to

recede, Longarm broke the kiss and drew a deep breath into his oxygen-starved lungs. This woman had taken it out of him in more ways than one, giving as good as she got. He nuzzled her throat, keeping his full weight off her with his elbows and knees until she tugged at him and whispered, "Please. Just stay there and hold me."

Longarm did as she asked, letting his weight down on her gently and tightening his arms around her. She kept her legs locked around his hips as she rocked a little side to side. His shaft was still buried deep inside her.

"That was so good . . . so good . . ." she breathed. Her hands stroked his back. Longarm lifted his head and kissed her chin, her nose, her eyes. She sighed contentedly. Then her eyes opened wider and she said, "Oh, Good Lord."

"What is it?" Longarm asked.

"I forgot to tell you my name. Lord, we haven't even been properly introduced!"

As soon as the words were out of her mouth, the timing of them must have occurred to her, because she began to giggle. The giggle became a full-throated laugh after a moment, and Longarm couldn't help but join her. He lifted himself slightly and said, "My name is Custis Long, ma'am, and I'm mighty pleased to meet you." His shaft, though softening now, gave a small throb inside her.

She caught her breath at the sensation, then smiled. "I'm Clarissa Harris," she said. "And I'm pleased to meet you too, Custis." She reached down and squeezed one of the cheeks of his backside.

Longarm chuckled again and said, "I reckon I ought to get off of you."

"I suppose so." Clarissa didn't seem all that happy about it, though.

Longarm rolled off her anyway and sprawled next to her on the bed. Her soft, pillowy breasts had spread out some on her chest in this position. He reached over and cupped the closest one, kneading the warm flesh. For her part, Clarissa reached down and fondled his manhood. Even soft, it was more than long enough and thick enough to fill the

49

palm of her hand. "I never knew anything could be so pretty, or feel so good," she said.

Longarm felt drowsiness overtaking him as he toyed with Clarissa's breast. He would have liked to doze for a while, then go at it again with her, maybe with her on top. He had a feeling she would be one hell of a bouncing handful. Bedding her in the first place might have been a mistake, though, he told himself. After a good romp like the one they'd just shared, he always slept soundly, and he couldn't afford to do that tonight, not with Sir Harry and Alice across the hall. He had to stay alert in case there was still somebody after the Englishman.

"I hate like the devil to say it, Clarissa," he began, "but I'm afraid you can't stay here—"

"Why not?" she broke in, startled. "I swear, Custis, I know you're leaving town tomorrow and I'm not trying to throw a rope over you. And I'm on my own, I promise I am. I don't have a husband or any brothers to come after you or anything like that. . . ." She ran out of breath.

Longarm shook his head and said quickly, "It ain't got anything to do with you, darlin'. But like you said, I'm a lawman, and I'm on an assignment here in Cheyenne."

"Those two English people you were with, that big gent and the lady—are they your prisoners?"

"Nope. But somebody may be after them. It's my job to protect them."

"You mean somebody might be gunning for them?"

"Could be," Longarm said, without going into any details about the three previous attacks on Sir Harry and Alice.

Clarissa sat up. "I hate to hear that. That fella seemed pretty nice, for a Britisher." She sniffed a little. "The lady looked a mite cold-natured, though."

Longarm wouldn't have said that, having kissed Alice and then watched her take her clothes off. But he couldn't very well tell that to Clarissa. Instead he said, "I have to look out for them, and I can't do that near as well with you here distracting me."

She ran a hand along his thigh and then closed her hand

around his shaft again. It was already starting to harden a little. "I can see that you're a man who's ... easily distracted."

"Depends on ... who's doing the distracting." Longarm grunted as Clarissa started pumping her hand up and down on his pole. Within a few seconds it was hard enough for her to swing a leg over his hips, straddle him, and sit down on it. It went up into her easily, since she was still so wet from before.

"Just a few minutes," she said as her hips began to move back and forth. "Just a few more minutes, Custis, please. That's all I want."

Longarm reached up and filled his hands with her breasts as she rode him. He reckoned he could spare a few more minutes, after all.

Watching Clarissa get dressed was almost as enjoyable as watching her get undressed. Almost. Longarm lay on the bed, wearing the bottom half of the long underwear again, as Clarissa pulled her dress on and fastened the buttons.

"Maybe I could come back early in the morning, before the dining room opens," she suggested.

"You're working the breakfast shift too?"

"I am tomorrow," she declared. "As long as you're going to be there. What about it, Custis? Do you want me to come back?"

Longarm wasn't sure how to answer that, but he was saved from having to by a sudden commotion in the hall. Somebody was banging a fist against a door, and from the sound of the disturbance, it was coming from right across the corridor.

From Sir Harry's room, in fact.

Longarm grated a curse and swung his legs off the bed. He leaped up and grabbed the Colt from its holster. Clarissa shrank back, moving out of his way as he hurried toward the door. Outside in the corridor, a man shouted, "Open up! Open up in there, I say! I know you are in there, Alice!"

What the hell? thought Longarm.

51

He jerked the door open, leveled his revolver at the man standing in front of Sir Harry's door, and said sharply, "Hold it right there, old son. You've raised enough of a ruckus."

The man stopped short with his fist upraised to hammer on the door again. To Longarm's surprise, he recognized the man. The troublemaker was the tall, lanky, wild-haired gent in the silk cloak that Longarm had noticed at the train station earlier in the evening.

The man looked over his shoulder at Longarm, and his eyes were just as wild as his tangled hair. "This is none of your business, *m'sieu*. It is between me and the woman whose beauty means the world to me."

Longarm heard the doorknob rattle and knew that Sir Harry was about to open the door. He called, "Sir Harry, don't!" But it was too late. The door swung open, and Blackstreet glared out at them. He was wearing a dressing gown over a tentlike nightshirt.

"What's going on out here?" he demanded. Then his eyes narrowed as he spotted the stranger. "Dumont!" he exclaimed. "What are you doing here, you madman?"

The man called Dumont drew himself up haughtily, still ignoring the fact that Longarm was pointing a gun at him. "I am here to reclaim my lost Alice," he said.

This fella sounded for all the world like a jealous suitor or cuckolded husband, Longarm thought. He said, "Maybe we ought to step out of the hall to palaver about this." Several doors up and down the corridor had opened slightly, and curious eyes were peering out as the guests tried to figure out what all the uproar was about.

Dumont sneered at him. "Who are you, some sort of servant? Stop waving that ridiculous gun about!"

Coldly, Longarm said, "I'm a United States deputy marshal, and in about half a second, old son, you're going to find out how ridiculous this gun is when I bend its barrel over your skull."

Dumont looked astounded. "You threaten me? Me, the greatest artist of our age?"

"To me you're just another loudmouthed son of a bitch who needs taken down a notch or two." Longarm paused, then added, "And I never heard of you before, mister."

That comment probably hurt Dumont more than clouting him over the head would have, which was why Longarm had said it. Dumont's face flushed with rage. He sputtered, "How . . . how dare you speak to me so, you . . . you American peasant!"

Longarm had had just about enough, so he didn't particularly mind when Dumont hauled off and took a swing at him.

He could have pistol-whipped the gent, but instead he easily ducked under the wild roundhouse punch Dumont threw. Stepping closer while Dumont was still off balance from the missed blow, Longarm grabbed his shoulder and jerked him around, then shoved him face-first into the wall. Dumont bounced off, his arms flapping crazily. Longarm kicked his feet out from under him, and as Dumont sprawled on the carpet runner in the center of the hallway, Longarm dropped on top of him, planting a knee in the small of his back and pinning him to the floor. Looking up at Sir Harry, Longarm asked, "Do you know who this lunatic is?"

Sir Harry sighed. "Unfortunately, I do, Marshal."

"Then I reckon he must be the one who's been after you."

"No, I fear that he is not," Sir Harry replied with a shake of his head. "This man is but a poor deluded fool who fancies himself an artist—"

"I *am* an artist!" Dumont practically screamed.

Longarm glanced toward the door of his room and caught a glimpse of Clarissa Harris peering out through the crack between the door and the jamb. It might be embarrassing for her if anyone else knew she was in Longarm's room, so to spare her that, he said, "Why don't we take this fella in your room, Sir Harry, and hash this out?"

"I suppose we must." To Dumont, Blackstreet added, "Phillippe, if Marshal Long lets you up, will you promise not to behave like the Gallic madman you are?"

Dumont sputtered something in French, probably a stream of cuss words, Longarm thought. But he was grimacing in pain at the same time from the big lawman's knee digging into his back, so after a second he nodded. "All right," he said. "But there is nothing to discuss. Alice's beauty is mine!"

"We'll see about that," Longarm said. He stood up, taking the weight off Dumont, who looked visibly relieved. Bending over, Longarm caught hold of the collar of the Frenchman's shabby coat and hauled him to his feet. "Get in there," he said, pushing Dumont toward the door of Sir Harry's room. He wished he'd had the chance to put his pants on, but it was too late for that now, and he wasn't going to leave Sir Harry alone with Dumont just because the only thing he was wearing was half a pair of long underwear.

Modesty was sometimes just a damned inconvenience.

Chapter 6

"Alice, go back to your room," Sir Harry said sternly as Longarm prodded Dumont along behind him into the hotel room.

Alice was wearing the silk wrapper again, but this time it was tightly closed. In fact, her hand went to her throat and pulled the garment even tighter around her as she saw Dumont. "Phillippe!" she exclaimed. "What are you doing here?"

"I came for you, *cherie,*" Dumont said, one hand rubbing his back where Longarm had knelt on him. "Did you think I would not?"

"I never thought you . . . you would follow us all the way to America!"

Sir Harry took Alice's arm and steered her toward the door of the adjoining room. "Marshal Long and I shall handle this," he assured her. "You have nothing to worry about, my dear."

"But . . . but Uncle—"

"Go on now, that's a good girl." Blackstreet practically pushed her into the other room and then shut the door firmly. His face was flushed with anger as he turned back toward Dumont. "How dare you follow us all the way across the Atlantic just to torment us?"

Dumont sniffed. "I come to torment no one. I simply want what is mine."

Longarm said, "Sounds to me like Miss Alice don't have any interest in being your lady friend, Dumont."

The Frenchman turned toward him, eyebrows arching in surprise. "Lady friend?" he repeated. "You believe that this is a matter of *l'amour,* an affair of the heart?"

"From what you've been saying, that's what it sounds like to me," said Longarm.

"But no!" Dumont exclaimed. "I want only Alice's beautiful body, I need her body!"

"Well, that's a mighty hard-hearted thing to say," Longarm responded with a frown. "I thought you French fellas were supposed to be so romantic."

Sir Harry sighed again. "You don't understand, Marshal. As I told you, Phillippe here fancies himself an artist. A sculptor, to be precise."

"A master sculptor!" Dumont corrected.

Sir Harry ignored him and continued. "He's been living in London, and Alice made his acquaintance somehow through friends. She foolishly agreed to pose for him, but before he could complete his sculpture, it was time for us to depart for America." Sir Harry glared at Dumont. "Needless to say, Phillippe did not take it well when Alice told him she would not be able to return to his studio."

"Art cannot be held to a timetable dictated by mundane life," snapped Dumont. "It follows its own schedule, and when the inspiration is flowing, it cannot be denied!" He clenched both hands into fists and shook them in the air.

"A mite excitable, ain't he?" Longram said to Sir Harry. "Are you sure he couldn't have had anything to do with those other ruckuses?"

"Ruckuses?" repeated Dumont. "What is this ruckuses?"

"Nothing to do with you, Phillippe," Sir Harry said quickly. "Now that you're here, what are we going to do with you?"

Longarm had been wondering the same thing himself.

"Allow Alice to return to London with me, so that I may finish my masterpiece," Dumont suggested.

"Impossible!" Sir Harry said without hesitation. "She is my niece, and she is traveling with me."

"Then I shall dog you every step of the way until you see the light of wisdom." Stubbornly, Dumont folded his arms across his chest and glared at Sir Harry.

"Not if you're in jail, you won't," Longarm said.

Dumont glanced a little nervously at him. "Jail? What have I done that would justify throwing me in one of your filthy American bastilles?"

Longarm supposed a bastille was the same thing as a hoosegow. He said, "How about disturbing the peace and assaulting an officer of the law?"

"I never actually struck you," Dumont pointed out.

"Not from lack of trying. And pounding on a door and hollering in the middle of the night is definitely disturbing the peace."

"Then take me before a magistrate and have me charged. I will pay my fine and be released before morning."

Longarm looked at Sir Harry and asked, "Can he do that? Pay a fine, I mean."

The Englishman nodded in resignation. "I'm afraid he can. Despite his habit of dressing like a beggar, Phillippe does have considerable financial resources. Some people seem quite taken with his work, though I, of course, am not one of them."

Dumont's lip curled in a sneer of triumph as he looked at Longarm.

Longarm stepped closer and said quietly, "Listen here, old son. I know the sheriff here in Cheyenne, and if I say so, he's liable to lock you up in the deepest hole he's got for a week or two before you ever see a judge."

That threat shook Dumont's arrogant facade. "That . . . that would not be legal!" he sputtered.

"Maybe not, and I'm sworn to uphold the law." Longarm paused, then added in a flinty voice, "So I would sure as

57

hell hate for you to make me do something that goes against the grain like that."

Dumont swallowed. "Will you not even allow me to speak to Alice, to plead my case with her?"

"Alice doesn't want to talk to you," snapped Blackstreet. "She just wants you to leave her alone."

"I would like to hear this from her own lips."

Sir Harry shook his head. "No. I want you to leave now, or else I will fully support Marshal Long's suggestion that we have you locked up."

Dumont's face took on a furtive aspect as he asked Longarm, "If I go peacefully, there will be no charges against me?"

A part of Longarm hated to let Dumont go after the fella had taken a swing at him, but that was what Sir Harry wanted. Longarm nodded and said, "That's right. No charges."

Dumont looked back and forth between them for a moment and saw nothing but angry resolve on the faces of both men. He sighed. "It appears that I have no choice but to accept your suggestion."

"Go then, and don't come back," Sir Harry said.

"Because if you do, I'm liable to shoot you on sight the next time," Longarm said, though he doubted if he would really do that. He had never minded bending a few rules and regulations, but he generally stopped short of gunning somebody down just because he was a pest.

Dumont straightened his clothes in a mostly futile attempt to regain some dignity. "Very well. I will go. But you have done a great disservice to the world of art by refusing to allow Alice to finish posing for me."

"I reckon we'll just have to struggle along without that statue of yours." Longarm took Dumont's arm and propelled him toward the doorway.

Dumont went grudgingly, but he went. He cast one last baleful stare toward Longarm and Sir Harry, then marched off down the hall without looking back.

When Dumont was gone, Blackstreet said, "I can't begin

to tell you how sorry I am about all this, Marshal. I never dreamed that Phillippe Dumont would follow us!"

Longarm still wished he had some pants on, but he wanted to discuss the Dumont situation with Sir Harry while he had the chance. Also, that would give Clarissa more of a chance to slip out of his room unobserved, if she hadn't already done so.

"Now that he's gone and we can speak plain about it, are you certain that fella couldn't have anything to do with your other troubles?"

Sir Harry shook his head. "As I indicated, Marshal, I'm positive. Dumont is a great annoyance, but he is not dangerous."

"I saw him getting off the train from Denver at the same time we did. That means he was in Denver this morning when those fellas jumped you at the art museum. The art business is another possible connection. If Dumont's as well heeled as you say, he could have hired those gunnies."

A frown creased Sir Harry's forehead, as if he had never thought of that possibility until Longarm had pointed it out, and he barked, "By Godfrey, you're right, sir! Dumont probably does have the funds necessary to do such a thing. But why? Why hire men to attempt to rob me and kidnap me, when it's really Alice he wants?"

"If you had been killed in any of those run-ins, Alice would have found herself on her own, a long way from home, with nobody to turn to. What would she have done under those circumstances if an old friend had shown up right then?"

Sir Harry clenched a hand into a pudgy fist and pounded it into the palm of his other hand. "The bounder! The absolute rotter! Of course Alice would have turned to him. I never would have thought that Dumont could be so ruthless, though. To . . . to employ murderers simply so she would come back and model for him once more!"

"Maybe there's more to it than that, no matter what he said," suggested Longarm.

"A romantic entanglement?" Sir Harry shook his head.

59

"No, that's impossible. The man's a catamite. Now, if Alice was a lad, I'd think you might have something there, but . . . no, definitely not."

Longarm scraped a thumbnail along the line of his jaw as he frowned in thought. If Sir Harry was right about Dumont preferring fellas to gals, then that left them with no motive other than the artistic one Dumont had claimed. Even though Longarm himself had suggested the theory that Dumont might be behind the attacks on Sir Harry, he wasn't completely convinced it was right. He was a long way from convinced, in fact.

But it was one more possibility, along with graft or some such at the mines that somebody was trying to prevent being exposed. Longarm supposed he would have to file it away in his head and wait to see what else developed.

In the meantime, he was tired of gallivanting around in his underwear. He bid Sir Harry good night for the second time and went back to his room.

Clarissa was gone. Longarm smiled faintly and shook his head. He hadn't expected her to still be here, but all the same, he felt a small sense of loss that was offset by the knowledge it was probably better this way.

Clarissa was all woman, and doing his job properly would have been a hell of a lot harder with her still around to keep him distracted.

Phillippe Dumont stood across the street from the Cattleman's Hotel and glared at the building. To think that he had been treated so ignominiously by that American lout. But then, all Americans were cretins.

The big *gendarme* was especially foolish if he thought that Dumont would really abandon his quest so readily. He would never give up until he had Alice back in his studio in London so that he could complete the statue of her he had begun. He would bide his time, Dumont told himself. Eventually, he would have his chance to speak to Alice alone again, and then she would understand how much he truly needed her.

"Got a match, mister?"

The voice took Dumont by surprise. He looked over and saw a stocky man who was several inches shorter than he was standing there on the sidewalk. The man wore a checked suit and a derby hat, and he had an unlit cigar clenched between his teeth.

"You were speaking to me?" Dumont said.

"I asked if you had a match." The man rolled the cigar to the other corner of his mouth. "For the stogie."

Dumont shook his head. "I do not smoke, and so I do not carry matches. So sorry." He didn't sound apologetic. He sounded as if yet another foolish American was bothering him.

The stranger didn't seem to take offense. He said, "Thanks anyway," and began to stroll away down the street. As the man departed, Dumont thought that he hadn't really sounded like the other men here in this frontier outpost, like the American cowboys and pioneers. Rather, he'd had a harsher accent, still definitely American but more like some of the street toughs Dumont had known in Paris and London. He wondered if the man came from one of the larger American cities back East.

Then he forgot completely about the man and went back to glaring balefully at the hotel.

After all, this chance encounter had nothing to do with art, and so was of no real interest whatsoever.

Frank Nickerson paused a block away and lit the cigar with a lucifer he took from his own pocket. The Frenchy wasn't paying any attention to him anymore, and therefore wouldn't think it odd that he had asked for a light when he already had matches. Nickerson shook out the flame and tossed the stub of the lucifer into the gutter.

Everything was going according to plan except for that French son of a bitch showing up. Nickerson had noticed him at the Cheyenne depot earlier in the evening, and now here he was again, watching the hotel where Blackstreet was staying with the girl and that lawman. Nickerson had always been a cautious man; otherwise he never would have survived all those years in the cutthroat arena of the Chicago criminal underworld. So he couldn't help but wonder if the Frenchy had some connection to Blackstreet.

It didn't really matter, Nickerson told himself. Things would work themselves out in time, and if the Frenchy got in the way . . .

Well, French blood was the same color as any other kind and would spill just as easily, Nickerson decided.

The rest of the night passed quietly, and Longarm was thankful for that. He dozed fitfully on the bed—with his pants on this time, in case he had to go rushing back out into the hall—and was up and fully dressed early. Clarissa didn't come back to his room, as she had said she might. Longarm couldn't help but be a little disappointed.

When he knocked on Sir Harry's door, the Englishman opened it and smiled out at him. "Good morning, Marshal," Blackstreet said. "I trust the rest of the night was as uneventful for you as it was for Alice and myself."

"Nothing happened," Longarm agreed. "I looked out in the hall a time or two during the night, but I didn't see that Dumont fella lurking around anywhere."

Sir Harry shook his head. "I think you put the fear of God into Phillippe. I doubt that we'll see him again. He'll probably slink back to London with his tail between his legs like the dog he is."

Longarm wasn't as convinced of that, but he was willing to wait and see. In the meantime, he said, "Where's Miss Alice?"

"She should be ready to go down to breakfast by now." Sir Harry crossed to the door of the adjoining room and knocked on it. A moment later, Alice opened the door and stepped into Sir Harry's room with a cheery smile.

"Good morning, Uncle," she said, then turned the smile toward Longarm. "Good morning to you too, Marshal."

Longarm tugged on the brim of his Stetson. "Ma'am." Alice certainly seemed to be in a good mood.

"I'm all packed and ready to go," she told Blackstreet.

"Excellent." He offered her his arm. "Shall we go?"

Longarm stepped back into his room, picked up his bag, and put it in Sir Harry's room with the other baggage to be taken to the train station. He tucked the Winchester under his arm and carried it downstairs himself. Cheyenne was more civilized than it had been a decade earlier, but its wild and woolly days were still recent enough so that a man carrying a rifle into a hotel dining room wouldn't be that unusual. In fact, hardly anyone paid any attention to it, Longarm noted as he strolled into the dining room a few minutes later with Sir Harry and Alice.

Clarissa was there, and she treated Longarm to a big smile as she showed the three of them to a table. Longarm glanced at Alice and saw the slight frown on her face. Alice's good mood had vanished, and Longarm had no doubt Clarissa was responsible. He tried not to sigh. He had enough on his plate keeping Sir Harry alive; dealing with the emotions of a couple of females who were interested in the same fella—him—was more than he wanted to do. It was a good thing they were leaving Cheyenne this morning.

The meal was good: ham and eggs and fried potatoes and biscuits hot from the oven so that wisps of steam rose from them when they were split open. Longarm and Sir Harry washed the food down with a pot of coffee apiece. Longarm kept pace with the Englishman for a while where the food was concerned, but Sir Harry finally surpassed him. An hombre would have to have a hollow leg to keep up with Blackstreet, Longarm thought.

When they were done, Longarm looked around for Clarissa, hoping to be able to tell her good-bye before they left. He knew that might put a bigger burr under Alice's saddle, but he didn't care. He'd grown fond of Clarissa in a short period of time.

The desk clerk in the lobby said to Longarm, "I had one of the boys take your things down to the depot, Marshal. The porters there will have them loaded for you."

Longarm nodded his thanks. "Train on schedule?" he asked.

"As far as I know, yes, sir, it is."

Longarm was glad to hear that. He was ready to move on to the next stage of the journey.

He caught a glimpse of something from the corner of his eye, and turned to see Clarissa standing on the other side of a potted plant in a little alcove off the lobby. She motioned for him to come over to her. Longarm frowned. He couldn't very well send Sir Harry and Alice on ahead to the station when his job was to protect them.

Sir Harry unwittingly came to his rescue by saying, "I believe I need to purchase some more tobacco before we leave. Where would I find the nearest tobacconist's shop?"

"Right here in the hotel, sir," the clerk said helpfully. He pointed to the other side of the lobby, where there was a counter behind which was an assortment of cigars and pouches of tobacco. The clerk came out from behind the registration desk. "I'll be glad to help you."

Sir Harry and Alice walked over to study the selection of tobaccos, while Longarm hung back and then stepped quickly and quietly over to the alcove where Clarissa waited. She caught hold of his hand and said, "I had to tell you good-bye, Custis. I hope I'm not causing a problem for you."

"The only problem I got is that it's liable to be a while before I pass through Cheyenne again and get to see you," he told her. "You take care of yourself, hear?"

"I will." She came up on her toes and kissed him, putting her hands on his face as she did so. "Good-bye, Custis," she whispered as she took her lips away from his.

Longarm turned away reluctantly—and saw Alice on the other side of the lobby, watching him. She must have seen Clarissa kissing him, because she was tapping the toe of one foot rather angrily. Longarm rolled his eyes. He asked himself whatever had happened to the days when all he had to worry about was a bunch of owlhoots trying to ventilate him.

Sir Harry concluded his transaction and tucked the pouches of tobacco he had bought into his coat pocket as Longarm rejoined him and Alice. "Shall we go?" he asked.

"I think it's more than time we did," Longarm answered honestly.

Chapter 7

Longarm inhaled deeply on the cheroot and blew the smoke out in a perfect ring that floated in the air of the railroad car for a few moments before dissipating.

"You do that quite well," Alice said from beside him.

"I've had a lot of practice. Been smoking these three-for-a-nickel cheroots for a long time."

Alice wrinkled her nose prettily. "I have to admit, they don't smell that much better than my uncle's pipe."

Longarm chuckled and said, "No, I don't reckon they do."

From across the aisle, Sir Harry Blackstreet weighed in with a loud snore. His head was drooped forward so that his double chins were more prominent than ever as he dozed.

The passenger cars on this train had bench seats. Longarm and Alice were sharing one, with Longarm beside the window, while Sir Harry had a seat to himself across the aisle. That worked out better for all concerned, Longarm thought, considering the Englishman's bulk. And he got to sit next to Alice this way. She had calmed down considerably in the two days since they'd left Cheyenne. She wasn't mad and jealous of Clarissa anymore, and she hadn't tried to seduce Longarm again. Of course, that would have been a mite difficult, traveling on a train like this, but he was sure she could have managed if she'd been of a mind to.

"My, those mountains are beautiful," Alice said as she leaned forward a little to look past Longarm out the window.

"That's the Humboldt Range," Longarm told her. "Pretty rugged country. I've chased owlhoots through it a few times."

"What an exciting life you must lead."

Longarm shrugged. "Don't know that I'd call it exciting. I stay busy, though, I'll say that much."

"I don't believe I've ever seen a country that can be so spectacularly beautiful and so spectacularly unappealing in such a short distance."

Longarm laughed and said, "Yep, most of the basins in Utah and Nevada ain't much to look at. They're dry and flat and hot, and if you ever find yourself afoot out there, you're almost as good as dead."

"Almost?"

"Well . . ." Longarm hesitated, then went on. "I recollect a time when some fellas who had a grudge against me dropped me down in the middle of the Great Salt Desert." He didn't mention that the Avenging Angels had left him there stark naked. "I managed to make it out, but it was a mighty near thing."

"You see, that's what I meant about an exciting life."

Longarm just shook his head. "It didn't seem too exciting at the time."

Alice was quiet for a few minutes, then said, "The most daring thing I've ever done was to pose nude for Phillippe Dumont."

"Nude?" Longarm couldn't keep from expressing his surprise.

"That's right," Alice said with a nod. "Phillippe said that all classical sculpture is of nudes."

Longarm grunted. "Maybe so."

"Oh, don't worry about Phillippe's motives. I'm sure Uncle told you that he's not, well, interested in women like that. Really, I think the only thing he's truly passionate about is his art."

Longarm hadn't seen hide nor hair of Dumont since they'd left Cheyenne. He hoped that meant the Frenchman had given up on his quest to persuade Alice to return to London with him. If Dumont had been behind the earlier attacks on Sir Harry, that would mean those were over too.

Alice looked over at Longarm with a sly smile. "Marshal Long, are you jealous that I posed nude for Phillippe?" she asked.

"I got no reason to be jealous," Longarm said flatly.

"Yes, but you've seen my body. Perhaps you don't like the idea that another man has seen it too."

Longarm looked around. Sir Harry was still sound asleep across the aisle, and no one else seemed to be paying attention to him and Alice. He said quietly, "I wouldn't go around talking about that if I was you."

"Why not? I'm not ashamed of my body. Didn't you like it?"

Longarm's teeth ground together for a second. She was doing this on purpose, he told himself, just trying to get under his hide. "I just think you ought to behave like a lady," he said, "so's you won't embarrass yourself or your uncle."

Alice laughed merrily. "I'm afraid Uncle is so far beyond embarrassment that nothing would bother him, Marshal. Unless it involved losing money somehow. He takes his finances as seriously as Phillippe takes his art."

Well, that was good to know, thought Longarm. In case of future trouble, he wanted to know as much as he could about the people involved in this case.

"When will we reach Virginia City?" Alice asked.

Longarm was grateful for the change of subject. He said, "We'll be there late this afternoon." It was already past midday, so he was only talking about a few more hours.

"Good. Riding on a train gets uncomfortable after a while."

That was true enough, Longarm supposed, although trains beat the hell out of traveling by stagecoach. As for himself, he would be glad to get to Virginia City too, because then maybe Alice would be distracted and stop teasing him.

A nude statue . . . Longarm wondered if Sir Harry knew about *that*.

Frank Nickerson reined in the horse he had rented in some godforsaken whistle-stop. He had cut across country from there, following the directions he had been given in the letter that had been waiting for him in Denver. His part of the plan was important, but he wished he had been able to accomplish it without having to bust his butt on some damned horse's back.

He had come to a stop some five hundred yards from the base of a butte that rose steeply on the edge of the foothills. Beyond the foothills were the Humboldt Mountains. At least, Nickerson fervently hoped they were the Humboldts. If they weren't, he was well and truly lost, and he might starve to death or die of thirst wandering around out here in the wilderness before he could ever find his way back to civilization.

The things a man would do for money, he thought as he took out a checked handkerchief and mopped sweat off his face. He lifted his derby from his head and wiped the inside of it too.

When he had clapped the hat back on his head and put the damp handkerchief away, he looked toward the butte again and saw the riders coming toward him.

There were at least a dozen of them, one man riding slightly in front of the others. As they came closer, Nickerson saw that the leader's hat had been cuffed back off his head to dangle from its chin strap around his neck. That exposed a wild thatch of dark hair that matched the thick beard on the man's face. He wore a blue shirt, stained dark with sweat, and a brown leather vest. Twin bandoliers with their loops stuffed full of cartridges crisscrossed his barrel chest. The butts of twin ivory-handled pistols, the only fancy things about him, jutted from holsters on his hips. He wore denim trousers and high, soft buckskin boots with fringed tops. He looked like something out of a dime novel, all right, Nickerson thought, but Harp Egan was the real thing, the leader of a genuine Western outlaw gang. One of the men who had ridden with him a few years earlier had wound up going east and becoming part of Nickerson's organization in Chicago, and when Nickerson had needed some Western help with this deal, Egan's old partner had been quick to suggest him.

The man brought his mount to a halt about ten feet in front of Nickerson, motioning for his followers to stop behind him. Nickerson swallowed and called, "Are you Harp Egan?"

"Are you Frank Nickerson?" the man responded in a deep, gravelly voice.

Nickerson smiled humorlessly. "I suppose the fact we know each other's name proves who we are."

"I reckon," Egan agreed. "Dooley Gibbons said you was one tough sumbitch." The outlaw leaned forward in his saddle, resting his left arm on the horn and giving Nickerson an ugly grin. "You don't look that tough to me. You look like a damn city boy."

Moving deliberately, Nickerson unbuttoned the single button that was holding his coat closed. "You want to find out how tough I am?" he asked, somehow managing to sound cool despite the heat.

It was a bluff, of course. If he reached for the gun on his left hip, he might be able to get it out before Egan could draw. Nickerson wasn't slow. He might even get off the first shot. With luck, he might actually kill Egan.

And then the rest of Egan's gang would fill him full of lead in about two heartbeats.

Or maybe it wasn't a bluff after all, Nickerson realized. He had lived his life being tougher and stronger than those around him. He was damned if he was going to back down to some filthy Western desperado.

Egan threw back his head and laughed. The other members of the gang, who looked almost as hard-bitten as their leader, followed suit. "I reckon you'll do, Nickerson," he said. "That letter ol'Dooley wrote said you had a job you needed help on. What are we goin' to do? Rob a bank? Grab a payroll or an ore shipment?"

"We're after something better than that," Nickerson said. "We're going to steal a goddess."

The train was still quite a ways northeast of Virginia City, but from the window by the bench where he sat, Longarm could see Mount Davidson rising in the distance. That was the center of the Comstock Lode, he knew, and the mining town lay on its lower slopes. Another hour would see them at their destination.

Up ahead, the rails made a long, sweeping curve to the left, crossing an arroyo on a high trestle. Longarm was looking idly toward the trestle when he saw it blow sky-high. Timbers went spinning crazily in the air, followed by a billowing cloud of dust.

Alice had dozed off, and was leaning her head against Longarm's shoulder. Across the aisle, Sir Harry had woken from his nap and was idly paging through a magazine. Both of them were jolted forward roughly as the engineer in the locomotive's cab saw the same explosion Longarm did and flung himself against the brake lever. In the instant following the blast, Longarm had known that the train would be coming to a violent halt, so he was able to brace himself on the back of the seat in front of him and keep from being thrown forward too strongly. He thrust an arm in front of Alice to keep her in her seat.

"Good Lord!" boomed Sir Harry. "What in the world—"

Screams of fear and shouted questions filled the car. Longarm surged to his feet and took hold of Alice's arm, helping her sit up straight again. She had gone pale, and he hoped she wouldn't faint.

"Stay here," he told her. "Sir Harry, keep an eye on Alice. I'll find out what's going on."

Longarm had a pretty good idea already. Blowing up the trestle like that could mean only one thing—somebody wanted to stop the train.

The cars were still shuddering as the drivers locked on the rails but kept skidding forward. Finally, the train came to a stop as Longarm took several long strides toward the door at the front of the passenger car where he and Alice and Sir Harry had their seats. The door flew open before Longarm could reach it, and acting on instinct, he palmed out his Colt and lifted it.

"Don't shoot!" squawked the conductor as he saw Longarm's gun come up and point toward him. He stopped just inside the door and raised his hands. "Are you one of the robbers?"

"No, I'm a U.S. marshal," Longarm snapped as he lowered the gun slightly. "What's happening?"

"Armed men came riding out from behind some rocks and headed for the engine. That's all I know." The conductor lowered his arms, took a deep breath, and seemed to gather a little courage around him. "I'm on my way to the express car. That's bound to be what they're after."

"You carrying any sort of special shipment?"

The conductor shook his head. "No, just the usual mailbags."

Longarm doubted that the outlaws were after what was in the express car then. It was true that a load of mailbags sometimes provided a hefty amount of loot, as did robbing the individual passengers at gunpoint. But he suddenly had a feeling that these owlhoots might be after something else.

He spun around to start back down the aisle toward Sir Harry and Alice, but before he could take more than a step, the door at the rear of the car was kicked open. A tall, burly, bearded man stepped inside, brandishing two six-shooters as he did so. He roared, "Nobody move!"

Longarm's fingers tensed on the trigger of his Colt.

Before he could fire, a grin split the leathery countenance

of the outlaw, who pointed his guns out to either side, almost like he was giving up. Longarm knew that wasn't the case, however. The outlaw's thumbs were looped over the drawn-back hammers of the guns. The barrel of the right-hand weapon was pointed at a woman and a little boy who cowered, terrified, in the rear seat on that side. To the left was a florid-faced drummer, equally terrified by the gun aimed at him. In an instant, Longarm took in the situation and knew that if he fired, even if he drilled the outlaw in the head, the man's thumbs would come off those hammers and somebody else would likely die.

"You got it figured right, hoss," the man called down the length of the car to Longarm. "You best drop that iron."

"Stop him," babbled the conductor behind Longarm. "You've got to stop him, Marshal."

"I can't do it without getting some innocent folks killed," Longarm said grimly. He took a deep breath.

"I'm getting tired of waitin', hoss!" bellowed the outlaw. "Maybe I'll just go ahead and shoot!"

"For God's sake!" burst out the drummer who was menaced by the train robber's left-hand gun. "Do what he says, mister!"

Longarm let his breath out in a sigh, then slowly bent over and placed his Colt on the floor of the car. He glanced at Sir Harry and Alice and hoped they understood that he didn't have any choice.

The outlaw's guns snapped forward again, pointing along the length of the car at Longarm. "That was mighty smart, hoss," the man said as he started to advance up the aisle. "Kick that gun under one of the seats where it ain't quite so handy, happen you get to feelin' foolish."

Longarm's booted toe nudged the Colt and sent it spinning under one of the seats.

"If you're here to rob us, old son," he said, "you'd best get on about it. Nobody has to get hurt."

"Well, now, that ain't quite what I got in mind." The outlaw's eyes were flicking from side to side, quickly studying each of the passengers he passed. He paused when he was one seat back from where Alice and Sir Harry were sitting on opposite sides of the aisle.

Longarm's jaw clenched. His hunch had been right. He was sure of it now.

But there still wasn't a damned thing he could do about it.

"I didn't stop this train to rob you good folks," the outlaw went on. "In fact, I just want one thing . . . and I reckon I see it now!"

With that, he abruptly holstered his left-hand gun and stepped forward quickly, reaching down to grab Alice's arm. She screamed as he jerked her out of the seat and onto her feet.

"By Godfrey, sir!" exploded Blackstreet. He came up out of his own seat with surprising speed for a man of his bulk.

But nowhere near fast enough. The gun in the outlaw's right hand lashed out and raked its barrel across Sir Harry's scalp. The blow was hard enough to make the Englishman slump back onto the bench, and blood seeped from the cut opened up by the gunsight.

"Stay down there, you stupid sumbitch! Get in my way and you'll get worse next time!"

"Uncle!" Alice cried shrilly.

The outlaw jerked her closer to him. "You shut up!" he snapped. "I don't like no gal screamin' in my ear less'n I'm pleasurin' her. Now come on along with me!"

"Please . . . you can't . . ." Sir Harry muttered. He was still stunned by the pistol-whipping he'd received.

The outlaw ignored him and started backing toward the door at the rear of the car. Longarm called after him, "I'll see you again, old son."

"The hell you will," grated the outlaw. "I've decided I don't want a gent like you on my backtrail."

He thrust his gun out, aiming directly at Longarm.

Longarm had no choice but to dive forward as the outlaw fired and hope the conductor behind him had the sense to get out of the way. The bullet whined over Longarm's head, and in the next fraction of time he heard it thud into flesh and heard the conductor grunt in pain. As Longarm hit the floor of the car, his hand was already snatching the derringer on the end of his watch chain out of his vest pocket. The length of the train car was farther than he liked to trust the accuracy of the little hideout gun, but he had to seize the only chance he had been given. Alice was still beside the outlaw, so Longarm had a clear shot at the man, at least for a second.

Before he could press the trigger, though, Sir Harry was in the aisle again, bellowing, "Alice! Alice!"

Longarm scrambled up. "Damn it, Sir Harry, get out of the way!" Down the aisle, Alice screamed again. Over Sir Harry's shoulder, Longarm saw the outlaw fire again, but this time the man was aiming into the ceiling of the car, and his shot accomplished its objective. The passengers panicked, and suddenly the aisle was clogged with people trying to get away from the shooting.

Longarm caught one more glimpse of the outlaw's grinning face before the man disappeared out the back door of the car, dragging Alice along with him.

Longarm tried to push past Sir Harry, and finally had to shove the Englishman out of the way. But he found more people blocking his path, and with a scowl of disgust gave up his attempt to follow the outlaw. Instead, hearing the pounding of hoofbeats, he leaned over to peer out one of the windows. He saw a dozen or so men riding hellbent for leather away from the railroad tracks. One of them was the big bearded outlaw, and he still had Alice with him. She was tucked under one of the man's arms, and though she was thrashing her arms and legs, Longarm knew she wasn't about to be able to break free of her captor's grip.

"Son of a bitch!" he said fervently.

"Marshal . . ." Sir Harry pawed at Longarm's sleeve. "Marshal, what happened? Where is Alice?"

"That owlhoot got away with her," Longarm said, and admitting it tore at his guts. "He must've had somebody holding his horse right outside. The whole gang took off for the tall and uncut."

75

"But why?" Sir Harry said. Blood was smeared on his forehead from the cut on his scalp. "Why would anyone take Alice? I thought *I* was the one they were after!"

Longarm had thought so too, so he couldn't answer Sir Harry's question. At the moment, he was certain of only one thing.

He intended to find out why those owlhoots had grabbed Alice—*and* get her back from them.

And if in the process he could put a bullet in that big bearded bastard, then so much the better.

Chapter 8

There was no way the blown-up trestle could be repaired. It would have to be completely rebuilt. Luckily, the gully it had spanned was not too deep, nor its sides too steep, to keep the train's passengers from climbing down, stepping across the trickle of water at the bottom, and climbing up the other side. Since a Western Union telegraph line ran alongside the railroad tracks, the engineer was able to shinny up a pole and cut in on the line to send a message to Virginia City requesting help. The conductor normally would have done that, but his shoulder had been busted by the bearded outlaw's bullet. Longarm had patched up the wounded man as best he could, utilizing the considerable expertise with bullet wounds he had picked up during his eventful career as a lawman. No one else had been hurt in the incident, except for Sir Harry, and the gash on his head had already stopped bleeding. Longarm bandaged it too.

It was nearly nightfall before a relief train came out from Virginia City pulling a baggage car and a couple of passenger cars. The passenger cars would be crowded, but everyone could get in. By that time Sir Harry Blackstreet was beside himself with worry.

"I don't understand, I just don't understand," he had muttered over and over as he paced up and down beside the tracks on the far side of the gully. Making the climb down into the gully and then out again had been difficult for him, but he had managed it. "I thought *I* was the one they were after!"

Longarm had figured the same thing. He had been more than a little surprised when the boss outlaw grabbed Alice instead of Sir Harry. And if the real goal was to have Sir Harry wind up dead, as Longarm had suspected it might be, that desperado had had several excellent opportunities to ventilate him. So there had to be something else behind the attack, something that made Alice important enough to carry off like that.

It was nearly dark by the time everyone was loaded onto the relief train, which then proceeded to back all the way to Virginia City. Night had fallen before the train got there, and a scattering of lights showed where the settlement sprawled across the lower slopes of Mount Davidson. All the streets slanted in Virginia City, Longarm remembered from previous visits, and a man couldn't go anywhere without walking uphill, downhill, or leaning to one side or the other.

The Storey County sheriff and a couple of railroad detectives were waiting at the solid-looking redbrick depot when the relief train backed in. They met the wounded conductor, who immediately pointed out Longarm and Sir Harry to them. The trio of grim-looking men intercepted Longarm and the Englishman before they could even leave the station platform.

"Marshal Long?" asked the man with the sheriff's badge pinned to his coat. "I'm Sheriff Reese." He jerked a thumb at the men with him. "This here's Hartley and Borden. They work for the railroad."

Hartley was a short, mild-looking man with thinning hair. Borden was taller and beefier, with brown hair under his high-crowned black Stetson. He said, "The conductor told us the outlaws kidnapped a lady who was traveling with you and your friend here."

"That's right," Longarm said. "Her name is Miss Alice Channing." He inclined his head toward Sir Harry. "This is her uncle, Sir Harry Blackstreet. They're visiting our country from England."

"You gentlemen have to help me recover my niece safely," Sir Harry said anxiously. "She means the world to me. Poor Alice! She must be terrified."

Hartley said, "I don't mean to pry, sir, but are you a wealthy man?"

"I have some financial resources, yes," Sir Harry replied with a frown.

"Then maybe those men kidnapped your niece in order to make you pay a hefty ransom to get her back," Hartley suggested.

The same idea might have occurred to Longarm if he had not known about the previous attempts to rob Sir Harry and then kidnap *him*. The railroad detectives weren't aware that the situation was more complicated than it appeared on the surface. Longarm decided that it might be better to leave them in the dark for the moment.

"I'll pay whatever they ask," Sir Harry declared. "I just want Alice returned safely to me."

"We'll do everything we can, Mr. Blackstreet," Sheriff Reese said. "What can you tell us about those owlhoots?"

"I . . . I only got a good look at one of the miscreants. He was a horribly ugly man, large and brutal-looking, with a beard and a veritable mane of dark hair."

Reese and the two railroad detectives exchanged a glance. "Did he wear crossed bandoliers and carry a couple of ivory-handled pistols?" asked Borden.

"That's the fella," Longarm confirmed.

"Damn it," Reese said. "That'd be Harp Egan."

"I reckon you know him?"

"I've been tryin' to put him behind bars for over six months now," Reese said.

"Dan and I have been trying to run him to ground too," Hartley said. "He and his gang have stopped several trains in Utah and Nevada and robbed them."

Borden said, "I'm surprised he only took Miss Channing this time. Egan must be counting on quite a ransom if he didn't even bother to rob the other passengers and blast open the safe in the express car."

Hartley was a shrewd bird, Longarm figured, and Borden, though younger and probably less experienced, seemed intelligent too. Sheriff Reese was a solid, competent lawman, but struck Longarm as not being overly imaginative. Longarm might have to bring the two railroad men in on the case sooner or later, but he still wanted to play a lone hand starting out.

He said, "We may have to just wait for this fella Egan to get in touch with us." By letting the others think he was going to be sitting on his backside, maybe he would have a chance to try to track down Egan on his own.

"Maybe," Borden said, "but we'll do some asking around and let you know if we come up with anything, Marshal."

"I don't care how you go about it," Sir Harry said. "Just find Alice and bring her back to me, gentlemen. That's all I ask."

But in the rugged mountains around Virginia City, thought Longarm, finding somebody like Egan who didn't want to be found might turn out to be quite a chore.

The first order of business was getting Sir Harry a room in the Truckee Hotel, one of the best hotels in town. When Longarm had the Englishman settled in a second-floor room in the impressive brick building, he said, "You just wait here and try to get some rest, Sir Harry. I'll be back in a little while, after I've done some nosing around."

Sir Harry was already pacing. "I don't see how I can possibly rest. Alice is missing, and I've a devil of a headache from the assault that damned hooligan perpetrated on me."

"He clouted you a good one, all right," agreed Longarm. "But you can't do Miss Alice any good if you're so worked up that you wear yourself out." A thought occurred to him.

"Do you want me to get in touch with the local boys who work for your mining syndicate?"

Sir Harry waved a hand. "I can't worry about that now. If the mine superintendent hears that I've arrived and comes here, that's fine. Otherwise, business can wait until Alice has been returned to me."

Longarm nodded. What Sir Harry said made sense, he supposed. He could see why the man wouldn't want to even think about business now.

"I'll see what I can find out," Longarm said as he paused at the door of the hotel room. "In the meantime, you stay right here, Sir Harry, and keep this door locked. Don't open it to anybody except me."

"I understand." Blackstreet hesitated, then added, "Marshal . . . this is all my fault, isn't it?"

"I don't reckon I know what you mean."

Sir Harry's voice was wretched as he said, "Somewhere, sometime, I did something to make an enemy, an implacable foe who is not going to cease his devilment until he has made of my life a living hell."

"It does seem like somebody's carrying a grudge against you, all right. You never heard of this Harp Egan fella before?"

"Never in my life," Sir Harry declared.

Longarm shrugged. "That don't surprise me. I expect we'll find that whoever the ringleader is just brought Egan in as a hired gun."

"Will he . . . will he harm Alice?"

Longarm grimaced briefly. "Hard to say. Most men out here in the West, even the owlhoots, won't hurt a woman. But there are always exceptions."

Sir Harry sank onto the edge of the bed, the mattress sagging under his weight, and put his head in both hands. "My poor Alice," he practically moaned. "My poor, poor Alice."

Longarm figured there was nothing more he could do here. He said, "Don't forget to lock the door," and left the room, heading downstairs.

The barroom of the Truckee Hotel was one of the most prominent watering holes in Virginia City. Longarm went in, found a place at the bar, and ordered a shot of Tom Moore. The bartender poured the drink from a bottle that was the real thing, and as Longarm sipped the rye, he judged that it was the genuine article too. He nodded his appreciation to the man behind the bar and half turned to look around the room.

For a hotel bar in a mining boomtown, the place was downright elegant, with gleaming hardwood panels on the walls, several chandeliers made of fine crystal, and booths with leather-upholstered seats around the walls. A poker game was going on at one of the tables, and Longarm recognized a couple of the players as mine owners, silver barons who could probably buy and sell the other men at the table several times over.

There were several females in the bar, but unlike typical saloon girls with heavily painted faces and short, spangled dresses, these women wore expensive gowns and hats and were only lightly made up. Longarm figured most of them could be had for a price anyway, but like everything else about the Truckee, they put up a more elegant front than was usually found on the frontier. One of the ladies stood up from the table where she had been sipping from a glass of wine and came toward Longarm. She had black hair and wore a dark blue dress and a hat of the same shade. The hat's brim dipped a little in front of her face.

"Hello," she said in a throaty voice as she came up to Longarm. "I don't believe I've had the pleasure of your acquaintance, sir."

"Custis Long, ma'am," Longarm introduced himself, leaving out the part about him being a U.S. deputy marshal. "And the pleasure of our acquaintance is definitely mine."

"I'm Grace Ellison." She slipped a gloved hand into his. "Mrs. Grace Ellison."

Longarm raised an eyebrow.

"I'm a widow," Grace went on.

"Sorry," Longarm murmured.

"It's been quite a while since my husband passed on, but I appreciate the sympathy, Mr. Long." Her hand was still in his, and she pressed his fingers as she spoke.

"What brings you to Virginia City?" asked Longarm.

"My late husband actually. He was a mine owner. He was killed in a cave-in several years ago."

Longarm didn't want to say that he was sorry again, so he just kept his mouth shut.

"Of course, that didn't happen until the mine had produced a sizable nest egg for us," Grace went on. "Not enough, however, that I wished to return to the East."

"So you decided to stay in Virginia City?"

"That's right. I found that I like it here, even though my friends back in Boston would be horrified that I actually prefer to live in such a crude frontier outpost."

"Virginia City's more civilized than some places out here," Longarm pointed out.

"It certainly is. But it still has a, shall we say, wilder side to it."

So, thought Longarm, what it amounted to was that Grace's husband had dragged her out here and then got himself killed in a mine that probably hadn't paid off nearly as well as he'd hoped before a few tons of rock fell on his head. That had left Grace without enough money to go home, but she'd had enough to buy a pretty dress and set herself up in business. She had been fortunate she was able to cater to a better crowd, rather than going to work in one of the cribs. That sort of life usually wore a woman out in a hurry.

Longarm didn't plan to bed her, at least not now, but he said, "Could I buy you a drink?"

"That would be very nice, Mr. Long."

"Custis."

"All right then . . . Custis. But you have to call me Grace." She gave him a seductive smile.

He was more interested in what she could tell him. He signaled the bartender, and Grace ordered a brandy. Again, the liquor came from a bottle that was genuine. She took a

83

sip and leaned closer to him, and he felt the side of her breast pressing softly against his arm. Maybe taking her up on what she was offering wouldn't have been such a bad idea after all, he thought, but unfortunately, he had work to do.

Longarm sipped his whiskey, then said, "I imagine a woman such as yourself hears a lot of talk, Grace."

Her tone contained just a hint of chilliness as she said, "What do you mean, a woman such as myself?" She might be a whore, but it was important to her that she not be reminded of it too blatantly.

"Well, I imagine you have acquaintances among the very best people in Virginia City."

"The very best," she agreed, looking somewhat mollified.

"Have you ever heard of a man named Harry Blackstreet?"

Grace frowned prettily in thought for a moment, then said, "No. No, I don't believe I have. Who is he?"

"Just a fella I know." Longarm didn't explain Sir Harry's connection to one of the mining syndicates. If Grace had already known who he was, that would have been different, but seeing as how she didn't, Longarm decided not to spread the information around. "What about Harp Egan?"

Grace's eyes widened in surprise. "Egan!" she exclaimed, though her voice was quiet enough so that it wouldn't be overheard easily. "He's an outlaw. A thief and a killer."

"Got any idea where I could find him?" Longarm asked casually.

Grace pushed away her half-full glass of brandy and said in a hard-bitten tone, "You've got the wrong idea about me, mister. If you're looking for Harp Egan, I don't want to have anything to do with you. Go down to the Alamo if you want the kind of woman who would associate with Egan."

That was what Longarm wanted to know. He put a hand on Grace's arm to stop her as she started to turn away. "I didn't mean any offense, ma'am," he said quickly. "I'm sorry if I've misjudged you."

"You most certainly have," she sniffed. But her angry attitude eased a bit. "You can make it up to me, I suppose."

"How can I do that?"

"Have a drink with me, up in my suite?"

"That's a mighty tempting offer, Grace . . . but right now I just don't have time."

She looked disappointed and still a little angry, and she said, "Are you sure? I could show you a very . . . pleasant evening."

"I imagine you could," Longarm said honestly. "Another time, all right? I expect I'll be here in Virginia City for a few days."

"All right then," Grace said. She reached back to the bar and lifted her brandy. "To pleasant evenings yet to come."

"I'll drink to that," Longarm said.

She was looking after him wistfully when he left the hotel barroom a minute later.

Longarm had figured that most of the soiled doves in Virginia City knew each other, and when Grace had approached him, he had taken advantage of the opportunity to learn where he could find a woman who might know something about Egan. It was likely that at least some members of Egan's gang slipped into Virginia City from time to time to have some fun and play a little slap-and-tickle, maybe even the boss outlaw himself. The saloon called the Alamo—no doubt owned by a Texan who had found himself in Nevada—was Longarm's destination as he walked down C Street. He remembered seeing the Alamo earlier, when he and Sir Harry were on their way to the hotel from the train station.

The boardwalk on this side of the street was a good foot higher than the one on the other side, due to the slope of the hillside. The Alamo was on the other side of the street, so Longarm was looking down on it as he approached. That might have been why he caught the flicker of movement behind the saloon's false front. He was passing under one of the gas streetlamps, which meant he was lit up almost as plain as day.

Instinct took over, sending Longarm in a dive toward the recessed doorway of the building he was passing. The store was closed for the night, but the alcove offered a little cover and some concealing shadows. Across the street, the whip-crack of a rifle shot sounded, and the bullet yelled through the space where Longarm had been an instant earlier.

He rolled deeper into the doorway and palmed out the Colt from his cross-draw rig. Tipping the barrel up, he fired twice, bracketing a second shot from the rifle. The bush-whacker's slug hit the streetlamp and exploded it, sending shards of glass spraying across the boardwalk. Longarm fired a third time.

No more shots came from across the street. Longarm didn't know if he had downed the ambusher or if the hombre had just decided to call it quits. He came to his feet, keeping his back pressed against one of the walls of the alcove. Along the street, people were emerging from build-ings and shouting questions, wanting to know what all the gunfire was about. Longarm suspected that Sheriff Reese or one of his deputies would arrive soon as well.

Nothing was moving behind the empty windows of the Alamo's false front now. Longarm was sure of that. He stepped out, holstered his gun, and picked up his hat, which had fallen off when he went diving for cover. He hit the Stetson against his leg to knock the dust off, then settled it on his head again and strode across the street toward the saloon. He wanted to avoid having to answer more ques-tions from the local law if he could.

Was it coincidence that somebody had tried to bush-whack him from the roof of the very saloon where he'd been going? Or had Grace passed the word to someone that he was heading down to the Alamo? That was pretty un-likely, Longarm decided. His conversation with Grace had been unplanned. There was no way Egan or anybody else could have used her to send Longarm into an ambush, and she'd had no reason to tip anyone off. He reminded himself that there was such a thing as coincidence in the world, even though as a lawman it was his natural inclination not to place too much stock in such things.

But then, if not for coincidence, Longarm thought a moment later, how else to explain the fact that Phillippe Dumont stepped out of the alley at the side of the Alamo, leveled a small pistol at him, and ordered, "Do not move, *M'sieu* Long."

Chapter 9

Now what the hell? Longarm asked himself as he froze at the edge of the boardwalk in front of the Alamo, where he had just stepped up to go into the saloon. His head was beginning to hurt from all the twists and turns of this case. He had thought—he had sure as hell hoped—that they had left Dumont behind for good.

Was Dumont the bushwhacker who had taken those shots at him just now? The Frenchman was holding a pistol, not a rifle, but he could have left the rifle on the roof of the saloon or in the alley.

"Hold on, old son," Longarm told Dumont. "You'd better put that gun down before you manage to land in some real trouble."

The barrel of the pistol trembled slightly, which meant that Dumont's hand was shaking. "Not until you tell me where I can find Alice," he said.

"You don't know where she is?" Longarm shot back at him.

"Of course not! Would I be pointing this gun at you if I knew? Do you think me an imbecile?"

As a matter of fact, Longarm thought the Frenchman was pretty damned addlepated, but now didn't seem to be the right time to point that out. Instead, he said grimly, "Alice was kidnapped off the train when it was held up a ways northeast of here. She was taken by an outlaw named Harp Egan."

Dumont began to shake even more, and he suddenly lowered the gun as a torrent of French came from his mouth. Longarm figured the words were curses from the sound of them. Dumont put his free hand to his face and said, "I did not know. I swear I did not know."

Funny thing was, Longarm found himself believing the man. He looked down the street, spotted Sheriff Reese hurrying along the boardwalk, and stepped over to Dumont.

"Put that gun away," he hissed. "Come on inside and have a drink with me."

"You . . . you mean it?"

"Yeah. Now come on," Longarm said urgently.

Dumont slipped the little pistol under his coat. Longarm took hold of his arm and steered him through the bat-wings and into the Alamo, which was a long, narrow room with a bar down the right-hand wall and a scattering of tables to the left. The saloon was about half full and buzzing with conversation about the shooting that had just taken place outside.

The bartender greeted Longarm and Dumont by saying, "Did you boys happen to see what went on out there? We heard some shootin', and there was some clumpin' on the roof like somebody was up there."

Longarm shook his head. "We heard the shots, but my pard and I didn't see anything. Did we, Phil?"

Dumont followed Longarm's lead by shaking his head and muttering, *"Non."* Longarm would have rather he'd answered in good old American rather than his native lingo, but the bartender didn't seem to notice.

"What'll you have?"

"A couple of beers," Longarm said. He wasn't holding out much hope that the beers would turn out to be particularly good, and when he sampled the stuff that the bartender put in front of him in a mug with foam slopping over the top of it, he found that he was right. The beer was weak and not the least bit cold. Longarm took a healthy swallow anyway, then pointed with the mug and said to Dumont, "Let's go sit down."

Dumont had to be reminded to take his beer with him. He and Longarm sat down at a table in a rear corner, and as they did so, Sheriff Reese came in. Longarm leaned forward, so that his hat brim was tipped down in front of his face. Maybe Reese wouldn't spot him, he hoped. He wanted to talk to Dumont privately.

Reese spoke to the bartender for a moment, glanced around the room, and then left the Alamo. Longarm heaved a sigh of relief, then said to Dumont, "Just so there's no misunderstanding, you didn't take a few potshots at me with a rifle from the roof of this place a few minutes ago, did you?"

"On my word of honor, I did not," declared Dumont. "I saw you on the other side of the street and was about to cross over and confront you, when you jumped into that doorway and started shooting. I heard the rifle shots, but had no idea from where they came."

Longarm glanced up toward the ceiling. "Somebody climbed on top of this building and opened up on me with what sounded like a Winchester."

Dumont shook his head and said, "It was not I."

Longarm was willing to accept that, at least for the time being. But there were still things he wanted to know. "Why'd you throw down on me?"

"Throw down? Oh, you mean threaten you with the pistol. So that I could force you to tell me the truth about Alice, of course. I did not see her with you and Sir Harry when you disembarked from the train, and I have been going insane with worry."

"How'd you get here ahead of us?"

Again Dumont shook his head. "I was not ahead of you. I was on the train as well. I knew that it had been stopped by brigands. But I had no idea that they had taken Alice. Ah, my poor *cherie*!"

He sounded a lot like Blackstreet, Longarm thought. Maybe the two of them had more in common than they would have thought. He commented, "You did a good job of staying out of sight. I looked for you on the train, and when I didn't see you, I figured we'd left you back in Denver."

"I have been with you every step of the way," Dumont said, his tone a little smug. "I paid the conductor to allow me to travel in the caboose with him."

So Dumont had bribed the conductor. Longarm considered briefly whether the powers that be at the railroad needed to know about that, and finally decided that they didn't. At least not if Dumont really turned out to be the semi-harmless eccentric he seemed to be.

"This is still about that damned naked statue, isn't it?"

Dumont drew himself up, clearly offended by the question. "It is a matter of art!"

"It is a matter of you being a burr under my saddle when I don't need one," said Longarm. "Look, Sir Harry was bound for Virginia City in the first place. I'll get Alice back from those owlhoots, Sir Harry will take care of his business here, and then I reckon they'll go back to England. Can't you pester them there instead of here?"

"You do not understand," Dumont muttered darkly. "You have no concept of the creative muse."

"What I got is a kidnapped woman and a bunch of outlaws to track down, and I can't do it with you dogging my trail. I told you back in Denver that I'd have you arrested if I have to. I can do that here too."

Dumont slumped back in his chair and glowered at Longarm. "Will you at least allow me to speak to Sir Harry?"

"Maybe," Longarm said. "But right now, I want you to just stay put." He drained the rest of the beer and then stood up to carry the empty mug toward the bar.

The bartender asked, "Another one?"

Longarm nodded and said, "Sure," even though the beer was piss-poor stuff. He went on. "You own this place?"

"Sure do."

"How long since you've been back to Texas?"

The bartender considered, screwing up his face in thought. "I make it nigh on to five years."

"I'd like to get back there myself sometime," Longarm said, even though two of his recent cases had taken him to West Texas.

The implication of Longarm's statement made the bartender's interest perk up. "Oh? You from Texas?"

"Waco," replied Longarm. He had been to that central Texas settlement enough so that he thought he could pretend it had once been his home.

"I'm from a wide place in the road called O-Bar. You probably never heard of it."

"Nope, I haven't," Longarm allowed.

"It's northwest of Fort Worth, sort of sits between two forks of the Trinity River. Pretty country."

"I expect so."

The bartender extended his hand across the bar. "Name's Nelson."

"Long," the big lawman introduced himself as he shook hands with the man.

"Pleased to meet you. Are you in Virginia City on business, just passing through, or did you come to get rich from the mines?"

"Business mostly," Longarm said. "What about you?"

Nelson laughed. "Can't you tell I'm a silver baron? I just run this place for the fun of it."

Longarm chuckled and said, "I won't let nobody in on your secret."

"I'd appreciate that. Let 'em all think I'm just a poor, hardworking saloon keeper."

Longarm figured he had laid enough groundwork. Nelson was feeling friendly toward him, considering him a fellow Texan. Longarm leaned forward over the bar and lowered his voice as he said, "I'm looking for a fella named Egan. You wouldn't happen to know him, would you?"

Nelson tensed visibly. "Egan? Never heard of him."

That answer had come back much too quickly, and besides, if Harp Egan and his gang had been holding up trains in the area, then Nelson certainly should have heard of him. The fact that Nelson had been so quick to deny even knowing who Longarm was talking about told the lawman that Nelson probably knew quite a bit.

"I'm not out to cause trouble for anybody," Longarm said. "And I ain't packing a badge." Now there was an out-and-out lie, he thought. "I just want to do some business with Egan."

Nelson's eyes flickered to the side, refusing to meet Longarm's gaze. The bartender wasn't just avoiding his eyes, however, Longarm realized after a second. Nelson was looking at something.

Or someone. Longarm glanced over his shoulder and saw a young woman sitting at a table with a couple of miners. She had dark skin and long, straight hair the color of a raven's wing. The high cheekbones indicated perhaps a touch of Indian blood. She wore a white blouse with a gathered neckline that swooped low in front, revealing the upper swells of her breasts, and she was undeniably lovely. She was also undeniably a soiled dove.

"Listen, mister, I told you, I don't know nobody named Egan," Nelson said. "And I don't want to have to tell you again." His friendly attitude had vanished.

Longarm shrugged casually. "I just thought, since we were fellow Texans and all—"

"I don't give a damn where you're from," the bartender cut in. "I don't know Egan."

"Fine. No offense meant."

Nelson didn't say anything.

Longarm drank the rest of the beer and set the empty mug on the bar. He dropped a coin beside it, then turned and went back to the table where Phillippe Dumont was waiting for him. Give Dumont credit, thought Longarm; the Frenchman hadn't budged while Longarm was talking to the bartender. But now, as Longarm rejoined him, he asked anxiously, "Did you find out anything?"

"Maybe. Don't know yet." Longarm indicated the mug

on the table. "Finish your beer and come on."

Dumont looked at what was left of the beer and wrinkled his nose. "This is swill! Have they no good wine here in this Virginia City?"

"I wouldn't know about that," Longarm said curtly. "Leave it and let's go."

Dumont left the beer where it was and followed Longarm out of the Alamo. Longarm's eyes flicked left and right as he stepped out onto the boardwalk, and his muscles were tense in anticipation of another possible attempt on his life. Nothing happened, though, as he and Dumont turned toward the Truckee Hotel.

"You will allow me to speak to Sir Harry now, no?" asked Dumont.

"Not just yet," Longarm told him. "Hang on a minute."

Longarm crossed the street, gesturing for Dumont to come with him. He picked a spot between streetlamps, where it wasn't quite as bright and the two of them might not be quite as noticeable. The hubbub over the earlier shooting had died down, and everything was back to normal. There were some people on the streets and the boardwalks, but Virginia City wasn't particularly busy.

Longarm reached the other side of the street, stepped up onto the boardwalk, and moved along it. Dumont came with him, muttering all the way. As they passed another darkened doorway, Longarm suddenly took hold of the Frenchman's arm and tugged him into the alcove. Shadows closed around them, shielding them from view.

"What are you doing?" demanded Dumont. "Why are we lurking here in the darkness?"

"Hush," Longarm ordered. "Just pipe down and let me keep an eye on that place."

"What place?"

"The one we just left," Longarm explained impatiently. He took his hat off and edged his head out so that he could peer back along the street toward the Alamo.

He had noticed while he and Dumont were in the saloon that it didn't have a back door. Unless somebody wanted to climb out a window, they would have to leave by the bat-winged entrance. Sure enough, Longarm and Dumont had been hiding in the doorway only a few minutes when a slender, shapely figure pushed through the bat-wings and stepped out onto the boardwalk. At this elevation, the nights were cool even in mid-summer, so the woman paused just outside the door to pull a shawl around her mostly bare shoulders. Longarm recognized the peasant blouse and the long, dark hair.

The woman leaving the Alamo was the same one the bartender had looked at when Longarm asked about Harp Egan.

That didn't have to mean a damned thing, Longarm reminded himself, but over the years he had learned how to read people pretty well. The bartender's glance at the soiled dove had been a small, instinctive reaction, but it had told Longarm a lot. It had told him there might be a connection between this woman and Harp Egan.

She strode along the boardwalk, moving purposefully, not just ambling. She met a man who put an arm out to stop her, but when he spoke to her, she shook her head emphatically, pushed past him, and went on. The man had asked her if she was looking for customers, Longarm figured, and she had said no, in no uncertain terms.

That meant she had somewhere to go and something to do.

Longarm glanced again at the Alamo. No one had followed the woman out of the saloon. In a quiet voice, he said to Phillippe Dumont, "Come on."

"Where?" Dumont asked testily. "I am tired of this. I wish to speak to Blackstreet."

"Later, old son. We got something else on our plate right now."

Longarm put his hat on and stepped out of the doorway. Dumont followed him with a sigh. Down the block and across the street, the young woman turned a corner and disappeared.

Longarm strode after her. He hoped that having Dumont

tagging along with him wouldn't ruin everything, but he didn't trust the Frenchman enough to turn him loose in Virginia City. Left on his own, Dumont would probably head straight for Sir Harry's hotel room and cause a ruckus.

The woman wasn't keeping an eye on her backtrail. Longarm was able to follow her without much trouble as she went to a small livery stable on the edge of town. The place was dark, but the woman pounded on the door until it opened and revealed a man in a nightshirt holding a lantern. He stepped back so that the woman could come in.

"Damn it," Longarm said. "I should've got my hands on a horse first." Horses, he mentally corrected himself, since Dumont would have to go along too.

"What are you talking about?" asked Dumont.

"I'm talking about a midnight ride," Longarm snapped. "Can I trust you to stay here?"

"And do what?"

"Just see which direction that woman goes when she rides off."

"How do you know she will be riding?"

Longarm reined in his temper. "Why else would she have come to a livery stable?"

"Is that what that hovel is? I had no idea."

"Look," Longarm said, "just stay here. I'll be back in a few minutes." He played his trump card. "If you keep an eye on the place and watch the woman, it may help us find Alice."

"Why did you not say so? Of course I will watch."

Longarm hoped Dumont was telling the truth. The man wasn't much of an ally, but at the moment he was all that Longarm had.

There were several other livery stables in Virginia City. Longarm had seen one of them on C Street earlier, and at the time it had been open. As he hurried toward it, he hoped it still was.

Luck was with him. The big double doors of the stable were closed, but a light was burning in the office window. Longarm rapped on the smaller door, and a balding man in shirtsleeves, suspenders, and trousers opened it a moment later. "Something I can do for you, mister?" he asked.

"I need to rent a couple of saddle horses," Longarm said.

The hostler frowned. "Kind of late to be takin' a ride, ain't it?"

Longarm opened the leather wallet that held his badge and bona fides. "This is law business," he said solemnly.

"Oh. In that case, come on in, Marshal, and I'll saddle up a couple of mounts."

"I'll help you with the saddles," Longarm said as he followed the hostler through another door into the main room of the barn. That would make things go faster.

Longarm estimated that a little less than ten minutes had passed since he'd left Dumont watching the other livery stable when he returned to the spot. He was leading the two horses so that they wouldn't make as much noise. "Dumont!" Longarm hissed.

"Here," the Frenchman said from the shadows. He moved forward.

"Did you see the girl leave?"

"*Oui,*" said Dumont. "She was riding a horse, just as you suspected she would be." Dumont sniffed in disdain. "Riding astride, as a man would ride. I think the lady is no lady."

Longarm didn't care about that. "Which way did she go?"

"There," Dumont said. He stepped out farther from the building and pointed to the great looming bulk of Mount Davidson.

Longarm nodded and said, "Mount up." He put a foot in the stirrup and swung up onto the back of one of the horses.

Dumont was hesitant. "I have never ridden one of these beasts."

Longarm sighed and thought, *Lord, protect us from tenderfeet—and foreign tenderfeet at that!* But he said, "Put your foot in the stirrup—yeah, that thing right there—and hold on to the saddlehorn. Pull yourself up and swing your other leg over."

Dumont managed to get on the other horse without being too awkward about it. Longarm handed him the reins. "Just do what I do." He heeled his own mount into motion.

Dumont followed suit, bouncing in the saddle even though the horse had a smooth gait. *"Merde!"* he said several times. But he was able to stay fairly close as Longarm rode out of Virginia City and started up the slope of the mountain.

"This is the way she went?"

"Oui."

Longarm's jaw was tight with tension. He hoped that the woman would lead him to Harp Egan's hideout.

And if she did, he realized, he might wind up having to ride right into the den of a bunch of desperate owlhoots with nobody to back his play but a damned crazy Frenchman who had never even been on a horse before.

Maybe Dumont wasn't the one who was really crazy after all, thought Longarm. That dubious honor might just belong to him.

Chapter 10

According to Dumont, the woman had left less than five minutes before Longarm returned with the rented horses. Up here in the clear, high mountain air, sounds traveled well, especially at night. Longarm called a halt once he and Dumont were well clear of the town, and he leaned forward a little in his saddle as he listened intently. After a moment, he heard the faint sound of hoofbeats.

"That way," he said, urging his horse forward again. Dumont followed, still clutching at the saddlehorn to steady himself.

Trailing someone this way wasn't easy, but Longarm had done it before and no doubt would again. His keen hearing made it a little less difficult. He was counting on the fact that the woman probably wasn't stopping to listen for the telltale sounds of anyone following her. She had a definite destination in mind, and Longarm hoped she was focused on that and nothing else.

Instead of heading straight up the mountain, the woman's route began to curve around the shoulder of the peak, skirting the big mining operations that were lit up, even at this time of night. Taking the silver out of the Comstock Lode deep under the mountain was a twenty-four-hour job.

Gradually, Longarm closed the gap between himself and Dumont and their quarry. He didn't ease up on the pace until he could actually see the woman in the silvery sheen of moonlight that washed down over the mountains. He hung back just far enough so that if she happened to glance behind her she wouldn't be likely to see him and Dumont.

They left the slopes of massive Mount Davidson and started along one of the many canyons that cut through the range of smaller mountains around the giant peak. There were mining camps up some of these canyons too, Longarm knew, and even some pretty respectable-sized settlements, but the canyon the woman followed was dark. The trail was choked with brush in places, and Dumont cursed under his breath as branches tore at his clothes and skin.

The canyon climbed to a pass between a couple of mountains. The woman stopped there, and Longarm caught sight of her, silhouetted against the lighter sky beyond, in time to draw rein and motion for Dumont to do likewise. They brought their mounts to a halt and watched.

Suddenly, light flared in the pass. It was small, no more than the flame of a match, but in those stygian surroundings, even the sputtering glare of a lucifer seemed bright. The woman lifted the match over her head and moved it back and forth three times before the little flame went out.

"A signal," Longarm breathed.

"What do you mean, a sig—"

"Ssshhh." Longarm didn't want any more noise than necessary. He and Dumont were about two hundred yards away from the woman, he judged.

Long minutes stretched out almost painfully. Then Longarm heard hoofbeats again, coming from the other side of the pass. Someone was coming in response to the girl's signal with the match.

Longarm would have been willing to bet it was either Harp Egan or one of the outlaw's men.

He leaned over and handed his reins to Dumont. "Hold the horses," he whispered.

"What?"

"Hold the damned horses," grated Longarm. "I'm going to see if I can get close enough to hear what they're saying." He slid out of the saddle. He didn't wait to see if Dumont was going to follow orders, but started cat-footing toward the pass instead.

Holding the horses was a simple job, but Dumont would probably foul it up, Longarm thought bleakly as he approached the rendezvous. By the time he was halfway to the pass, he could see that a man on horseback had joined the woman. Longarm had to move carefully so as not to make any noise, and he buttoned his coat so that his watch chain would be covered and couldn't reflect any stray beams of moonlight.

The newcomer didn't look big enough to be Egan, and as Longarm drew closer and settled down behind a clump of brush to eavesdrop, he began hearing the man's voice and knew it wasn't the boss outlaw's gravelly growl. This man's voice was higher-pitched and irritated as he said, "Damn it, Juanita, you know you're supposed to stay in town less'n Harp sends for you."

"I have news," the soiled dove—Juanita—said. "A man is in Virginia City looking for Harp. A lawman, I think, and Nelson agrees."

The outlaw laughed. "Hell, lawmen been lookin' for Harp for months now, and they ain't even come close to him. You got spooked for no reason, gal."

Juanita tossed her head angrily. "Harp told me to come and tell him if I found out anything important. I thought he would want to know about this man. Why did he not come to meet me himself?"

"Because he's already in Virginia City tonight, damn it! If you had just stayed there, you likely could have told him about that law dog yourself."

Longarm stiffened. Egan was in Virginia City? Why, after blowing up a railroad trestle, stopping a train, and kidnapping Alice that afternoon, would Egan venture into Virginia City tonight?

Sir Harry was back there alone, Longarm thought as a cold chill went through him.

"You might as well get on back there," the outlaw went on to Juanita. "I'll tell Harp about the lawman. You know his name?"

"He told Nelson that his name is Long."

"What sort of law is he?"

"I don't know. A federal marshal perhaps."

That was a good guess, thought Longarm. Juanita had a sharp eye for star-packers.

She was curious too, because she asked the same question that had occurred to Longarm. "Why would Harp go into Virginia City?"

"He said he had to deliver a message to a fat Englishman."

"What?"

"Don't you worry your head about that, gal. Just get on back to town. Maybe you'll run into Harp on the way."

A fat Englishman. There was only one man in Virginia City that could be: Sir Harry Blackstreet. Longarm bit back a groan. He had hoped to provoke somebody in the Alamo into leading him to Egan's hideout, and that plan had worked pretty well. But in doing that, he had left Sir Harry alone and pretty much defenseless back in Virginia City, and Egan had gone there after him! Grimacing, Longarm began to back away.

He heard the woman say, "Harp had better not have stopped to see some other girl while he was in town."

"Don't worry about that," the outlaw said with another laugh. "The only gal ol' Harp's interested in right now is one called the Golden Goddess."

Longarm paused again. Golden Goddess?

What the hell?

Dumont was waiting with the horses, right where Longarm had left him. The Frenchman was pretty irritating, but at least he followed orders part of the time. Longarm motioned for Dumont to stay quiet, then took the reins of his horse from him and swung up into the saddle.

Longarm was torn about what to do next. He wanted to get back to Virginia City as soon as possible to check on Sir Harry, but he didn't want to tip anyone off that he had a lead to Egan's hideout. It was somewhere on the other side of that pass, close enough so that a lookout could easily see the signal Juanita had given. Even though the delay chafed at him, Longarm decided that he and Dumont would wait until Juanita had passed before starting back to town.

Dumont was about to burst with questions, Longarm sensed. He gestured for the Frenchman to keep his mouth shut, and they sat there in silence, hidden in the brush, until Juanita had ridden past them and disappeared down the canyon. When he judged that she had enough of a lead for it to be safe for them to move, Longarm nudged his horse forward and hissed to Dumont, "Let's go."

"Did you find out anything about Alice?"

"Not really, but I've got a hunch I might be able to find Egan's hideout now," Longarm replied.

"Then why are we going back to Virginia City instead of rescuing Alice?" Dumont demanded irritably.

"Because that's where Egan is, and I reckon there's a good chance he's after Sir Harry."

"I care only about Alice—" Dumont began.

"Well, my job is to protect Blackstreet," Longarm cut in. "I don't like leaving Alice in the hands of those owlhoots any better than you do, but I have to try to stop Egan from whatever devilment he's up to."

"I could go back and look for Alice. . . ."

"And get you and her both killed, more than likely," said Longarm. "Stick with me, Dumont. I'm the best chance you've got of getting Alice back safely."

Longarm hoped he was right about that.

Dumont's complaints subsided, and he rode in silence as Longarm led the way back to Virginia City. They didn't have to worry about staying on Juanita's trail now, so Longarm was able to take some shortcuts and set a little faster pace. They skirted Mount Davidson and rode toward the sprawl of lights that marked the settlement.

Longarm went straight to the hotel instead of stopping at the livery stable where he had rented the horses. As he and Dumont rode up to the building, Longarm didn't hear any shooting or yelling or any other sort of ruckus, and he hoped that was a good omen. Maybe Egan hadn't been able to get to Sir Harry before now. Dismounting quickly, Longarm looped the reins around the hitch rack in front of the hotel and stepped up onto the boardwalk, not waiting to see if Dumont did likewise. He strode into the lobby. Everything seemed peaceful. The clerk behind the desk glanced up and gave Longarm a pleasant nod.

Longarm relaxed a little, but not entirely. He went to the stairs and took them two at a time as he climbed to the second floor. Dumont was behind him, hurrying to keep up. Longarm grabbed the newel post on the banister at the second-floor landing and swung around to start down the hallway toward Sir Harry's room.

At the far end of the corridor was a window, and climbing through that window was Harp Egan.

Longarm didn't know if Egan was coming or going. He and the outlaw spotted each other at the same instant, and both men reached for their guns. At the same time, Longarm thrust his other arm back and shoved Dumont against the wall of the staircase, out of the line of fire. He palmed out the Colt and snapped a shot at Egan. The slug chewed splinters from the window frame not far from the outlaw's head. Hard on the heels of Longarm's shot, Egan's revolver boomed and sent a bullet whining past the lawman's head. Longarm went to the floor in a rolling dive as Egan fired again.

The Colt bucked in Longarm's hand as he fired a second time. Egan vanished from the window, but Longarm couldn't tell if the outlaw was hit or had simply dropped out of sight. He scrambled to his feet and ran down the corridor, and as he approached the window he heard the rapid thudding of hoofbeats. Egan must have dropped to the alley where he had a horse waiting.

Aware that he was making a target of himself, Longarm thrust his head and shoulders out the open window and looked around. The sound of the running horse was diminishing. The alley was empty. "Damn it!" Longarm grated. Egan had made his getaway.

There was no blood splattered on the windowsill. Longarm had missed the outlaw with both shots.

He turned back and saw a pale-faced Dumont standing at the top of the stairs. The Frenchman seemed to be uninjured, just spooked by the shooting. He started toward Longarm as the lawman strode toward the door of Sir Harry's room. Other doors along the hall were being opened cautiously as hotel guests looked out to see what all the commotion was about, but Sir Harry's door remained shut.

Longarm was afraid of what he was going to find in there.

The stink of powder smoke hung in the air of the corridor. Dumont said anxiously, "That man . . . he was the brigand, no?"

"He was the brigand, yes," snapped Longarm. He still had his gun in his right hand, so he used his left to pound on Blackstreet's door. "Sir Harry! Are you all right?"

There was no response from inside. Longarm muttered a curse and reached down to grasp the knob. He twisted it and shoved.

Sir Harry Blackstreet was sitting on the edge of the bed, Longarm saw immediately, in almost the same position he'd been in when Longarm left earlier in the evening. The Englishman was still fully dressed. Longarm didn't see any blood on his clothes. "Sir Harry!" Longarm said sharply. "Are you all right?"

Sir Harry looked up at Longarm with dull eyes. He had a piece of paper in his hand, Longarm noticed now. "Someone . . . someone pushed this under the door," Sir Harry said, his voice as stunned as his gaze.

Longarm stepped over to him and reached down to take the paper out of the Englishman's pudgy fingers. The paper was brown and grimy, and it looked like it might have been used to wrap meat at some time in the past. But the letters printed crudely on it with a piece of charcoal were easy to read:

If you want the girl back alive, bring us the Golden Goddess. Three Pines, dawn.

Longarm scanned the words, then said bleakly, "Look at me, old son."

Slowly, Sir Harry raised his eyes until they met Longarm's cold gaze.

"It's time for the truth," said Longarm. "It's time you told me all about the Golden Goddess, Sir Harry."

First, though, there was the matter of all the attention the shooting had drawn. Several people had seen Longarm stalking down the hall with a gun in his hand, and they had seen him go into Sir Harry's room as well. So there wasn't going to be any avoiding the sheriff's questions this time, Longarm knew.

Sure enough, less than a minute after Longarm had demanded the truth from Sir Harry, a determined knock sounded on the door. Dumont, who had followed Longarm into the room and closed the door behind him, now opened it at Longarm's gesture to do so. Sheriff Reese stood there, a shotgun in his hands. He looked comfortable holding the Greener, as if he had used it plenty of times before.

"Thought you might have something to do with this, Marshal," Reese said as he stepped into the room. "You want to explain why you were shootin' up the hotel a few minutes ago?"

"Harp Egan was here," Longarm said bluntly. He inclined his head toward Blackstreet. "I think he must've planned to come gunning for Sir Harry." Longarm didn't mention the ransom note, which he had folded up and put in his pocket.

106

"Egan!" exclaimed the sheriff. "Right here in Virginia City?"

"I got a good look at him, and I ain't likely to have forgot him since this afternoon. It was him, all right."

Reese cursed. "And you swapped lead with him?"

"We both missed," Longarm said. "At least, I know he did, and I'm pretty sure I didn't ventilate him before he got away."

"Son of a bitch!" Reese looked at Dumont. "Who's this feller?"

"A friend of ours," Longarm said quickly. That was stretching the truth a mite, but he was convinced now that Dumont didn't have anything to do with the trouble that had been plaguing Sir Harry. He couldn't imagine that there would be any sort of connection between the Frenchman and an outlaw like Harp Egan. "He saw Egan too."

"Is that right?" asked Reese.

"I saw an ugly man shooting at Marshal Long from the window at the end of the hall," Dumont replied. "I do not know the man's identity, but if Marshal Long says he was this brigand Egan, then I am certain he was."

"All right," Reese said, turning back to Longarm and Sir Harry. "But you don't know for sure why he was here?"

"Nope. All I know is he saw me and went for his gun, so I figured I'd better do likewise."

Reese nodded. "A man don't have much choice in a case like that." He rubbed his jaw and then asked shrewdly, "You didn't happen to have somebody take a few shots at you earlier tonight, did you? Down around the Alamo Saloon?"

Witnesses could place him in the Alamo too, Longarm thought, so he said, "I was there talking to Dumont here, but we came along right after the shooting. Folks in the saloon were still talking about it, though."

The sheriff grunted. Longarm couldn't tell if the local lawman believed him or not. But Reese couldn't prove that Longarm wasn't telling the truth, so for now there was nothing he could do about it.

"No offense, but you seem to bring trouble with you, Long. Why do you reckon that is?"

Longarm just shrugged and said, "I don't know, Sheriff. I'm a peaceable man."

Reese grunted again and nodded, but it was clear he thought there was more to the story than Longarm was telling him. He said, "I hope the rest of the night ain't quite so eventful."

"You and me both, Sheriff. You and me both."

Reese left, still wearing a suspicious frown. When the door was shut, Longarm turned back to Sir Harry and found him staring at Dumont.

"You," Sir Harry said. "What are you doing here?"

"I have come to rescue my fair Alice," Dumont said. "Someone must protect her, since it is obvious you cannot."

Sir Harry growled and started to get to his feet, but Longarm put a hand on his shoulder and pushed him back down on the bed. "You and Dumont can hash things out later," he said. He took the ransom note from his pocket. "Right now, we got to talk about this—and about the Golden Goddess."

Sir Harry hesitated, then rubbed a hand wearily over his face and sighed. "You're right, Marshal," he said. "The time has come for the truth."

Chapter 11

"It's a fabulous story, sir, utterly fabulous," Sir Harry began, "and it goes back hundreds of years."

"In that case," Longarm said as he reversed one of the straight-backed chairs in the room and straddled it, "maybe you'd better not start at the beginning."

"But I must if you are to understand," Sir Harry protested.

Longarm gestured resignedly for him to go on.

The Englishman leaned forward slightly. "This all began in the days of the Renaissance, in Italy. A powerful nobleman who was also a patron of the arts commissioned a sculptor to create a statue of the nobleman's mistress. It was to be a present, you see, for the woman, who was married to another nobleman. What made the statue special was that it was crafted out of pure gold."

"Nonsense," Dumont interjected with a sniff. "Gold is much too soft to make a proper statue."

"This was a figurine, not a full-sized sculpture," Sir Harry snapped. "And it was made of gold and decorated with precious gems."

"Thing like that ought to be worth a pretty penny," drawled Longarm.

"Indeed! A small fortune. But the nobleman could afford it, as he was also one of the leading merchants in all of Italy." Sir Harry began to warm to his topic. "Unfortunately, the mistress's husband discovered the relationship, and being a jealous, hot-tempered Mediterranean sort, he followed his wife to one of her trysts with the other fellow and burst in on them *in flagrante delicto*."

"You mean while they were romping betwixt the sheets?"

"Exactly. The cuckold, having a dagger with him, promptly used it on both of the lovers, then took the Golden Goddess and presented it to *his* mistress. She, unfortunately, was killed a short time later when she was trampled by a runaway team of horses pulling a cart."

"What happened to the figurine?" asked Dumont.

"Those deaths were only the beginning of a long chain of murder, accident, and illness that claimed the lives of many of the owners of the Golden Goddess," Sir Harry said. His voice dropped ominously. "Within a century, it began to be bruited about that the figurine was cursed. But it was still extraordinarily valuable too, so men continued to desire it. When a man wants something badly enough, he will run any risk."

Longarm knew that was true.

"Finally, the Goddess was brought to London to be placed in a museum there, but when the curator dropped dead, it was decided that the statue would be sold instead. I outbid a Russian fellow who was also after it."

"You are not afraid of the curse?" Dumont asked.

Sir Harry waved a hand in dismissal of such things. "I am not a man who is easily frightened. Besides, I never planned to keep the Golden Goddess. I was coming to America anyway, so I contacted a man I knew would be interested in purchasing the figurine. He even sent a man to London to bid in the auction, but the representative was delayed and arrived there too late. The Goddess was already mine."

"So you figured on selling this statue once you got to the States," Longarm said.

Sir Harry nodded. "Precisely. In fact, the gentleman who arranged to purchase it from me is supposed to meet me here in Virginia City to complete the transaction."

Longarm came to his feet. "You've got the Golden Goddess with you?" he asked tersely.

Sir Harry took a deep breath, then nodded. "Yes. Of course I do. How else could I turn it over to the man who's purchasing it?"

"And that's what those gents have been after all along?"

"It's . . . possible. The Russian fellow I mentioned before did not take kindly to being outbid. He could have hired men to steal the figurine. In fact, I'm fairly certain that's exactly what he did. One of the men who accosted us in Chicago . . . well, I happen to know that he is a leading figure in the criminal underworld there. His name is Frank Nickerson."

"How in blazes do you know that?"

"I was told the man's identity by a private detective I hired. Nickerson seems to be well known in Chicago."

Longarm started to pace back and forth. "You knew all of this all along?" he asked.

"Well . . . yes."

Longarm turned sharply toward him. "You son of a bitch!"

Sir Harry's eyes widened, and his face flushed with anger. He was unaccustomed to being spoken to in such a tone, but right now, Longarm didn't give a damn.

"If anything happens to your niece, it's your fault for keeping me and my boss in the dark about this," Longarm went on angrily.

"I simply needed protection until I could conclude my arrangement with the man who is purchasing the Goddess," Sir Harry returned coldly. "I thought your government could provide that without having to be privy to all the details of the situation."

With an effort, Longarm reined in his temper. A part of

111

him wanted to tell Sir Harry Blackstreet to go to hell. But Alice was still in danger, still in the hands of Harp Egan's gang.

"This fella Nickerson—he could have followed you out here and hooked up with Egan and his bunch?"

Sir Harry shrugged. "That seems a likely theory to me."

"And Egan was the one who slipped that ransom note under your door, because Dumont and I damned near caught him in the act."

"Again, that makes sense."

Dumont spoke up. "You have to give them what they want. You must save Alice."

"Blast it, I can't do that! The Golden Goddess is worth a fortune!"

"Let's see it," said Longarm.

"There's really no need—"

"I want to see this geegaw," Longarm said. "Now."

Sir Harry stood up and went to one of the bags that was sitting in a corner of the room, casting an angry glance toward Longarm as he did so. But he bent over and rummaged through the bag, coming up with a package wrapped in plain brown paper.

He set it on the room's dressing table and began tearing away the paper. Underneath the paper were several layers of thick cloth that had been wrapped around the object they concealed. Sir Harry unwound the cloth, and suddenly the light from the lamp reflected dully off a polished surface that came into view. After a moment's work, the paper and cloth lay around the feet of the golden figurine they had protected.

"My God," breathed Phillippe Dumont. "It's lovely."

Longarm had to agree. He had seen several statues of naked women back in that Denver art museum, but what he was looking at now in a room in the Truckee Hotel in Virginia City was just as pretty.

The Golden Goddess was a little over a foot tall, and perfectly proportioned. The woman's features were exquisitely detailed, as was her body. The breasts thrust forward, high and proud, and were tipped with tiny rubies. More gems were set around the figurine's neck like a necklace, and around each wrist to form bracelets. Sir Harry turned the little statue around slowly, giving Longarm and Dumont a good look at it. The sculpting was very realistic, right down to a dimple in the middle of one cheek of the statue's rump.

"Nice," Longarm commented. "But it doesn't look like something so many men would die over."

"Most men are willing to die for beauty, in one for or another," Sir Harry murmured.

Longarm reached out and wrapped a hand around the figurine. "Well, there's only one thing we can do. We've got to trade this trinket to Egan and Nickerson for Alice's life."

"No!" Sir Harry burst out. "The Golden Goddess is mine, and I refuse to turn it over to those . . . those scoundrels! You'll just have to think of another way to rescue Alice, Marshal."

Longarm frowned. He might be able to find Egan's hideout, but there was no guarantee of that. And even if he did, he couldn't count on getting Alice out of there alive. He'd been willing to give it a try when there seemed to be no other way to proceed, but now that another opportunity had presented itself . . .

"I didn't say we'd let Egan and Nickerson keep the blasted thing," he said. "But if they're going to have any gal in their hands, I'd rather it was this golden one. Once we've got Alice back safe and sound, I'll track down the gang and get the statue back."

"How can you be so sure that you will recover the Goddess?" Sir Harry demanded.

"Well, I'll do my dead-level best—"

Blackstreet was already shaking his head. "No. No, I simply cannot allow it. The figurine is too valuable."

Longarm's jaw tightened. He wasn't in the habit of stealing folks' property from them, but if he had to take the Golden Goddess in order to improve the chances of successfully rescuing Alice, that might be what he had to do. He was disgusted with Sir Harry for putting money above the life of his niece, or mistress, or whatever she really was, but some gents were like that. Longarm had been a lawman too long to be really surprised by anything people did.

He looked down at the little statue in his hand, and was about to tell Sir Harry where he could put the thing once he'd recovered it, but then the Englishman suddenly brightened and said, "I have an idea."

"It had better be a good one," growled Longarm.

Sir Harry leveled a finger at the Frenchman. "Dumont."

"*Moi?*" Dumont said in surprise.

"What about him?" asked Longarm.

"Loath though I am to admit it, Dumont *is* a sculptor of some small repute."

Dumont looked like he was about to argue with that small-repute business, but Longarm motioned for him to be quiet.

Sir Harry clasped his hands behind his back and began pacing back and forth as he spoke. "What if Dumont were to create another statue? A duplicate of the Golden Goddess that would be essentially valueless?"

Dumont couldn't restrain himself this time. "My work always has value!" he snapped.

"But not like the Golden Goddess," Sir Harry said. "Consider, Marshal. Nickerson is a common criminal, and this man Egan is a Western variation of the same thing. Both of them could be easily fooled by a duplicate, and by the time the fake reached their employer, who is in Constantinople, it would be too late to do anything about it. Alice would have been safely returned to us long before."

Longarm scraped a thumbnail along his jawline as he thought about Sir Harry's idea. It was sort of a harebrained scheme, he decided, and yet it still might work. Sir Harry was right about Nickerson and Egan not being art experts. But surely, if they had been hired by the Russian collector Sir Harry had mentioned, the man might have given them some way of telling if the figurine was authentic.

"It'd be a long shot," Longarm said dubiously.

"But it might succeed," Sir Harry pressed him.

Longarm had to shrug and nod his head. "Crazier things have happened, I reckon."

Sir Harry spread his hands. "There you have it. We'll start immediately."

"Start how?" asked Longarm. "How long will it take Dumont to make a duplicate statue? And can he even get what he needs to do it here in Virginia City?"

"The statue could be sculpted of lead with only a thin coating of gold," Sir Harry said. "And we would need some small, cheap gems to substitute for the real things. Surely those items would be available?"

Dumont put in, "And as for the time involved, I could work quickly. My artistic skill is such that it would not take a great deal of time. Twenty-four hours perhaps. Perhaps even less." Clearly, he was warming to the challenge, and he had another motivation as well. "I would do anything for Alice. My lovely Alice."

Longarm thought Dumont was being mighty passionate about Alice, considering that all he wanted her to do was pose for him. But each fella had his own particular passions, Longarm reminded himself.

He mulled it over for another moment, then abruptly nodded. "All right," he said. "We'll give her a try." He took the folded ransom note out of his pocket and held it up. "But according to this, Egan and Nickerson will be expecting us at dawn at someplace called Three Pines. They'll want the Goddess then."

Dumont shook his head. "Even if I work all night, I will not be finished by then."

"You must meet with those men, Marshal Long, and persuade them to wait," said Sir Harry.

"Stall them, you mean."

"Precisely."

Sir Harry was right. Longarm didn't have any artistic talent to speak of, unless you wanted to count being a pretty fair hand with a whittlin' knife, but there was one thing he knew how to do, and that was dealing with bad men. Come morning, he would have to ride out to meet Egan and Nickerson at Three Pines, wherever that was.

And hope that he came back alive.

The first thing Longarm did was clatter back down the stairs to the lobby and head over to the desk. The clerk looked at him and asked, "Something I can do for you, Marshal?"

"Tell me where I can find some lead, some gold, and some cheap jewelry," Longarm said. "Then tell me how to find a place called Three Pines. And keep your mouth shut about all of it."

The clerk's eyes widened. "Is this law business?" he asked breathlessly.

Longarm nodded curtly. "It sure is." The clerk was impressed to be asked to help out a lawman. Longarm hoped the man wasn't the talkative sort.

The clerk nodded eagerly. "Go on down to the assay office. It'll be closed for the night, but Pliny Jones—he's the assayer—sleeps in the back. Just pound on the door and wake him up, but you'll have to knock pretty hard because he's a sound sleeper. You ought to be able to get some lead and some gold from him, as long as you don't need too much."

"I'll need something to melt the gold too," Longarm said.

"Pliny can help you out with that, more'n likely. Now, as for the jewelry, there's a place that sells it over on B Street. Just go a block past the assay office, turn left, then turn right at the next corner."

Longarm nodded, filing the directions away in his head.

"You can get anything you want there, but you'll have to wake up the owner, just like at the assay office," the clerk went on. "His name's Joe Monahan. Tell him I sent you down there. He sells good stuff to the silver barons for their ladies, and cheaper jewelry for everybody else."

That sounded just like what Longarm needed. "What about Three Pines?" he asked.

"Take the Reno Road north out of town. It follows the

railroad for a while, then swings off to the west for a ways. About two miles farther on, you'll see a hill off to the west with three pines on top of it. That's all, just the three pines. That's where the name came from."

"I'm much obliged," Longarm said as he placed a coin on the desk.

The clerk slid it back across to him. "No, sir, Marshal, you don't owe me a thing. I'm just glad I can help out the forces of law and order."

"You can help even more by keeping quiet about this," Longarm reminded him.

"Mum's the word," the clerk said, but Longarm didn't really believe him. He figured that within a day or two the man would be bragging about how he'd helped out the law. But maybe by then Alice would be back safely.

Longarm left the hotel and started on his errands. Pliny Jones, the assayer, proved to be just as difficult to wake as the clerk had said he was, but Longarm finally managed after several minutes of banging his fist against the door of the assay office. The door was jerked open, and a bearded face glared out at him in the light of a candle held by the man. Jones wore a nightshirt and boots, and his mouth was sunken in because he had taken out his false teeth for the night. "Who're you, and what'n hell do you want?" he demanded thickly.

"U.S. Deputy Marshal Long," Longarm introduced himself, "and I need some lead and gold and the tools to work them."

Jones stared at him for a moment, then declared, "You're drunk! Who put you up to this?"

Longarm had his badge ready. He held it up so that Jones could see it in the candlelight. "It's no joke," he said grimly.

"Well, then, come on in," the assayer said grudgingly. "I'll see what I can come up with."

Less than an hour later, Longarm used the back door to return to the hotel, so that folks wouldn't notice him coming in with several heavy crates. He had a couple of handfuls of cheap jewelry stuffed into his pockets too. With the supplies he'd rounded up, Dumont might be able to fashion a passable duplicate of the Golden Goddess, Longarm thought. As Sir Harry had pointed out, the fake wouldn't have to fool any experts, just a passel of owlhoots.

"Excellent! Simply splendid!" Sir Harry said, rubbing his hands together in anticipation when Longarm had carted everything up to the hotel room.

"I shall get to work immediately," said Dumont. He practically dived into the crates, bringing out a gas burner and a pot for melting the gold, followed by large chunks of lead and smaller pieces of the dully gleaming metal that was the gold.

"I'm going across the hall to get some sleep," Longarm said. "I'll have to leave before dawn to get to Three Pines on time."

Dumont shook his head. "How can anyone sleep while Alice is in danger?"

Longarm would have expected to hear such sentiments from Sir Harry, but the Englishman made no comment. Instead, he just sat and looked at the Golden Goddess, which he had set on the table so that Dumont could study it as the duplicate was created.

Longarm went back to his room and took off his hat, coat, vest, tie, gun belt, and boots. Still wearing the rest of his clothes, he stretched out on the bed and dozed off with the ease of a man accustomed to taking his sleep wherever and whenever he could get it. His slumber was light, though, and he woke up well before dawn. After getting dressed again, he went across the hall and knocked softly on the door.

Sir Harry opened it. The Englishman was beginning to look a bit less dapper than he usually was. His clothes were rumpled, and his eyes were bloodshot from lack of sleep. Beyond him, sitting at the table working on the fake statue, Dumont also looked somewhat haggard. Longarm stepped into the room and closed the door. He studied the ugly thing on the table in front of Dumont.

The Frenchman had heated the lead and fused several chunks of it together into a single irregular piece that was a foot and a half tall. It didn't resemble anything remotely human, Longarm thought. If Dumont could take that hunk of lead and make it look like a beautiful woman, then maybe he really did have talent.

"The work is going well," Sir Harry said. "I take it you're going to keep the rendezvous with Nickerson and his outlaw cohorts?"

"That's the idea," Longarm agreed. "Anything else you need before I ride out?"

"Time," muttered Dumont as he leaned forward in his chair and used some sort of tool to scrape away a few flakes of the lead. "Time to create."

"I'll stall Egan and Nickerson as long as I can," Longarm promised.

It was early enough that the hotel dining room wasn't open yet. A different clerk was dozing behind the desk, and he didn't wake up as Longarm walked quietly through the lobby and stepped out onto the boardwalk. The horses Longarm and Dumont had used the previous evening to follow Juanita from the Alamo were still tied at the hitch rack. Longarm took their reins and led them down the street toward the livery stable. He paused along the way to pick up a couple of biscuits at a small cafe that opened earlier than the hotel dining room. The biscuits were hard and probably left over from the night before, but he could gnaw on them on the way out to Three Pines, Longarm told himself. It was better than nothing. When he got back, he could have a regular breakfast with a pot of coffee.

The hostler was already up and around at the livery stable. Longarm turned the horses over to him and asked for a fresh mount. The hostler saddled and brought out a chestnut gelding, and Longarm nodded his head in approval. He grasped the horn, put his foot in the stirrup, and swung up into the saddle. With a touch of his heels, the horse trotted out of the stable.

Longarm turned north on the road that ran to Reno, up

in the valley of the Truckee River. He wasn't going as far as that settlement, however. He was just going to Three Pines.

The sky in the east was turning gray now. Dawn wasn't far off. Egan and Nickerson would be waiting at the appointed spot, Longarm was sure of that.

With any luck, they wouldn't shoot him when he told them that he didn't have the Golden Goddess—at least not yet.

Chapter 12

Longarm generally preferred sunsets to sunrises, but he had to admit that the array of colors in the sky was spectacular this morning as the blazing orb began to peek up over the sawtoothed peaks of the Humboldt Range.

Black shaded into dark blue, dark blue into purple, purple into a profusion of orange and gold. Light spilled over into the valley where the railroad and the trail ran. The trail had already veered away from the tracks, just as the hotel clerk had said it would. Longarm knew it couldn't be much farther to Three Pines.

A few minutes later he spotted the hill a couple of hundred yards off to his left. Brush covered the lower slopes, but it was mostly bare rock until the very top, where three good-sized pine trees had somehow taken root. From a strategic standpoint, Longarm admired the choice of location for the rendezvous; if Nickerson and Egan and their men were already atop the hill, as seemed likely, they could cover all the approaches. Nobody would be able to make it up those open slopes unless that was what the outlaws wanted.

Longarm clucked to the chestnut and hauled on the reins.

The horse left the trail and started across the sage-littered flats toward the hill.

The sky grew brighter and brighter as the sun rose behind Longarm. Having the sun behind him was the only possible advantage he might have if this meeting deteriorated into a gunfight, and it was only a small edge. And if it came to that, Alice's chances for survival would be pretty slim too.

As he rode toward the hill, Longarm kept an eye on the top of it, watching for the telltale glint of the rising sun's rays off metal. Sure enough, a moment later he saw a flash from the hilltop and felt certain it was the reflection off a gun barrel. Instinct told him to turn around and ride the other way. Either that, or haul his Winchester out of the saddle boot and dive off to hunt some cover. Instead of doing either of those things, he kept going, drawing closer and closer to the hill called Three Pines.

He reached the strip of brush at the bottom, which wasn't as thick as it looked from a distance. Longarm started up the slope, urging the chestnut through gaps in the brush. A few minutes later they broke out into the open once again.

As they did so, a rifle cracked somewhere up above and a bullet smacked into the slope, kicking up dust and splinters of rock a short distance in front of Longarm and the horse. Longarm reined in as the horse shied nervously and tried to dance sideways. As he brought the chestnut under control, a voice called from the top of the hill, "That's far enough!"

Longarm stayed where he was, sitting in the saddle with both hands in plain sight. He had recognized the rough voice that had called down the command. It belonged to Harp Egan.

There was nothing Longarm could do now except wait and see what Egan wanted him to do next. That wasn't long in coming.

"Show us the Golden Goddess!"

Longarm took a deep breath and called back, "I don't have it!"

Every muscle in his body was tense. Even though it was

early in the negotiations, this was a crucial moment. Egan and Nickerson might decide that if he didn't have the statue, his life was forfeit. Longarm was poised to dive out of the saddle if bullets started to sing around his head.

There was a long stretch of strained silence, then Egan, still unseen somewhere on top of the hill, bellowed, "What do you mean, you don't have it?"

"Sir Harry wouldn't let me bring it!" Longarm shouted. "Not until you prove that the girl is still alive!"

That was logical enough, and as a stalling tactic, it just might work. Longarm could claim that he couldn't bring the statue out here until he had seen Alice with his own eyes, then returned to Virginia City to deliver the news to Blackstreet.

A rifle blasted again, and Longarm was about to throw himself out of the saddle until he realized that the slug had struck the hillside a good ten yards to his right and whined off harmlessly.

"You son of a bitch!" howled Egan. "You think we're bluffin'?"

The shot had been meant to spook Longarm, and to show him that the outlaws meant business, he thought. And probably so that Egan could blow off a little steam too. Still keeping his hands halfway lifted, Longarm called, "You'll get your statue, mister! But I've got to see the girl first!"

Again there was silence from the hilltop. Longarm could imagine that there was a heated discussion going on up there. Egan might be in favor of killing him, but Nickerson would be arguing in favor of accepting that condition if it meant they would get their hands on the Golden Goddess. Or maybe it was the other way around; Longarm didn't really know the personalities of the men involved. All he knew was that Harp Egan had struck him on the train as a hothead, the kind of man who shot first and then tried to sort things out later.

"Stay there!" Egan yelled again after several more moments. "Don't you move, damn it, or we'll fill you full of lead!"

"I ain't going anywhere, old son," Longarm called back.

He lowered his hands and crossed them on the saddle horn, leaning forward slightly to ease the muscles in his back. He waited while the minutes stretched out unpleasantly. He wasn't fully convinced that Egan and Nickerson hadn't planned on pulling a double cross all along, but he had figured that they at least would have Alice with them.

Finally, Longarm saw movement on top of the hill. Two men rode out from the pine trees and down the slope a few feet. One of them was Egan. Longarm had no trouble recognizing the fierce, bearded features of the boss outlaw. The other man on horseback was smaller but still stocky and muscular. He wore a town suit and a derby hat, and Longarm immediately pegged him as Frank Nickerson.

Most of Longarm's attention, however, was focused on the figure on foot between the two horses.

Alice's hat was gone, and her blond hair was loose around her face and blowing a little in the early morning breeze. Her dress was rumpled and torn. She stood straight, though, with pride and anger evident in the way she carried herself. She looked awfully pale, but Longarm reminded himself that she was fair-complexioned to start with.

"Well, here she is!" shouted Egan. "You satisfied now?"

Longarm cupped a hand to his mouth and called, "Miss Alice! Are you all right? Have they hurt you?"

Alice didn't answer until Egan nudged her with a boot. "I'm fine, Marshal Long!" she called down the hill. "Just very tired and very frightened!"

Egan left Alice and Nickerson where they were and spurred his horse on down the hill toward Longarm, halting when he was only about twenty yards away. "All right, you badge-totin' bastard," he grated. "You've seen the girl. Now go get that damned statue."

Longarm thought quickly. "It'll be tonight, about sunset, before I can get back with it."

"Sunset!" exclaimed Egan. Curses tumbled out of his mouth for a moment before he went on. "It don't take anywhere near that long to ride to Virginia City and back!

What the hell are you tryin' to pull?" The boss outlaw jerked out one of his pearl-handled revolvers and pointed it at Longarm. "You think we're fools?"

"I think you're smart enough to know that these things sometimes take time," Longarm said coolly—a lot more coolly than he really felt inside. "Sir Harry doesn't have the statue. It's coming in today on the westbound train, and that trestle you blew up yesterday won't be repaired until late this afternoon." He had turned the blame for the delay around and pinned it on Egan.

Again, the outlaw turned the air blue with profanity, concluding by saying, "That Englishman wouldn't let the statue out of his sight!"

Nickerson edged his horse forward and called, "That's exactly the sort of thing Blackstreet would do. He's a tricky son of a bitch."

Egan turned his head and glared at his new partner for a second, then asked, "You sure about that?"

Nickerson said to Longarm, "Does Blackstreet want that girl to die?"

"Of course not," Longarm replied.

"Then you'd better have that statue back out here by sunset," Nickerson said. "Otherwise the deal's off and he'll never see the girl alive again."

"I'll be here with it," vowed Longarm.

Egan looked mad and frustrated, but there was nothing he could do. In the eyes of his partner, he was just as much to blame for the delay as Blackstreet was. He jammed his gun back in its holster, pointed a finger at Longarm, and said, "You try to double-cross us and I'll see that you wind up dead too, mister."

"Nobody's going to double-cross anybody," Longarm said calmly. "And nobody has to die."

Egan just grunted and wheeled his horse around. He galloped back up the hill, pausing long enough to snatch Alice up and throw her across the horse's back in front of him. They disappeared over the crest of the hill, followed by Nickerson.

It was hard for Longarm to let them ride off like that with Alice, but at least he had bought some more time, he told himself as he turned his own mount and started riding slowly down the hill. The skin on his back crawled a little, and he knew that several members of the gang probably had their rifles trained on him. Gradually, the feeling died away as he reached the bottom of the hill and urged the chestnut into a trot that carried them back toward the trail.

Longarm lifted a hand and wiped away the beads of sweat on his forehead. Now it was all up to Phillippe Dumont and that duplicate statue he was making. . . .

The sun was well up in the sky by the time Longarm reached Virginia City again. The streets were busy, and the sounds of the stamp mills reducing the ore from the Comstock Lode to its component elements filled the air. Longarm rode straight to the Truckee Hotel and left the horse at the hitch rack in front. As he stepped up onto the boardwalk, he caught a glimpse of a couple of familiar figures on horseback down the street. They turned a corner and disappeared, but not before Longarm recognized them as Hartley and Borden, the two railroad detectives. Longarm frowned slightly, wondering if the two men had been following him. He hadn't noticed anyone on his backtrail, but that didn't mean they hadn't been there. Most of Longarm's attention had been focused on finding Three Pines before dawn.

He went inside, telling himself he was worrying about nothing. Hartley and Borden had been on Egan's trail for quite a while; if they had followed Longarm to Three Pines and seen the outlaw out there, surely they wouldn't be back here in Virginia City. They would be trying to track Egan to his hideout, since they knew nothing about the ransom demand.

Or did they? They must have seen Alice as well as Egan and Nickerson, thought Longarm. And they would have witnessed the conversation between Longarm and the two criminals. It wouldn't take much thinking on their part to put all that together and come up with a good idea of what was really happening.

Longarm grimaced. He had no proof that the railroad detectives had been following him. There was no point in borrowing trouble.

Still, he told himself he would keep a closer eye behind him next time.

Sir Harry opened the door in answer to Longarm's knock. If the Englishman had looked tired the last time Longarm saw him, by now he was positively exhausted. But not as exhausted as Dumont, who looked up with hollow, dark-ringed eyes from the table where he was working on the substitute statue.

"Did you see her?" Sir Harry demanded immediately, even before he'd completely closed the door. "Did you see Alice?"

"I saw her," said Longarm. "She's all right. She said they hadn't hurt her, and I believe her. They'll want to keep her in reasonably good shape until they get their hands on the Golden Goddess."

Sir Harry rubbed a hand over his face and heaved a sigh of relief as he sank down on the edge of the bed. "Thank God," he said. "I was afraid they might have killed her out of hand."

"Nope. They'll take care of her—until they get the statue," Longarm said again. "Then I reckon all bets are off."

Sir Harry looked up at him. "What do you mean by that?"

"They're liable to try to double-cross us and kill both Miss Alice and me before we can get away."

"But . . . but you are going to take them the statue!" Dumont said from the table.

"A phony one," Longarm pointed out.

"They will not know that!"

"Even if they think it's the real thing, they might still decide to try to kill us," Longarm said. "But I'll do my best to see that they don't."

"Of course," Sir Harry muttered. He didn't look as encouraged as he had a moment earlier. The realization that this was far from over was sinking in on him, Longarm thought.

The big lawman stepped over to the table and looked down at what Dumont had accomplished so far. The hunk of lead, which had looked like nothing human before, now had a semblance of a woman's shape to it. The curves went in and out where they were supposed to. But all the details, the features of the face and body, were still missing. Not to mention the fact that the thing was all still lead.

"I told Egan and Nickerson that I'd have the statue back out there at Three Pines by sunset," Longarm said. "That was as far as I thought I could push them. Can you have it ready by then?"

"I . . . I do not know. . . ." Dumont straightened in his chair and squared his shoulders. "*Mon dieu!* What am I saying? Of course I can have the statue ready. I must, for Alice's sake!"

"Well, then, don't let me stop you," Longarm said. He took off his hat, tossed it on a side table, and sat down in an armchair to wait and smoke.

He lost track of how many cheroots he went through that day. All he knew was that it was a lot. Exhaustion finally claimed Sir Harry, as the big man slumped back on the bed and started to snore for a while. Dumont continued working feverishly. His face seemed to become more drawn and gaunt as Longarm watched. Dumont refused to stop working even to eat when Longarm brought trays up to the room from the hotel dining room. The man drank some coffee with a splash of brandy in it, but that was all.

From time to time during the afternoon, Longarm stalked over to the window and pushed the curtain aside enough to peer out at the street. Virginia City seemed to be going about its business normally. No one else knew about the desperate race with time that was going on in this hotel room. Longarm kept an eye on the sun as well, charting its inexorable course across the sky.

Dumont fired up the burner again and began to melt the small pieces of gold in the pot suspended over the flames. Longarm looked at the lead statue and saw to his surprise that other than its dull gray color, it looked almost exactly like the Golden Goddess. He looked from one figurine to the other, comparing them, and saw only minute differences.

"You've done a hell of a job, Dumont," he said.

"Yes," agreed Sir Harry, coming closer. "Superb work, Dumont."

"I had no choice," Dumont said without looking up from what he was doing. "Alice's life is at stake." After a moment, he said, "I must have a bigger pot, something big enough so that I can put the figurine in it and pour the gold over it."

"I'll see what I can do," Longarm said. He headed downstairs to the hotel kitchen.

The cook was reluctant to hand over a clean stew pot, but Longarm flashed his badge and took it anyway. He'd apologize later for being a mite high-handed, he told himself. Right now there wasn't time to worry about hurt feelings. It was getting on toward late afternoon.

The stew pot worked fine. Dumont stood the lead figurine upright in it and using leather gloves to hold the other pot, carefully poured the molten gold over the fake statue. Enough of it stuck to the soft lead to form a thin sheath. What ran off was scraped up by Dumont, heated again, and poured over the figurine once more. The process was repeated several times until the little statue had a uniform coating of gold on it.

"That thing's probably worth a thousand bucks or more," Longarm commented as he looked at the statue. "If we don't get it back and wind up having to pay that assayer for the gold we used, my boss ain't likely to be happy."

"A thousand dollars!" Sir Harry snorted with a dismissive wave of his hand. "A grain of sand on a beach compared to the true worth of the original!"

129

"Maybe, but the cost of this one is liable to come out of the government's pocket."

"Don't worry, Marshal. I will be glad to reimburse your government for any expenses incurred in rescuing Alice."

Longarm nodded. "All right. Maybe with any luck we won't have to hold you to that. I still plan to see Egan and Nickerson behind bars, so they can't cause any more ruckuses."

What he didn't mention was that men such as Egan and Nickerson usually didn't surrender peaceably to the law. That was why most of them wound up dead instead of in the hoosegow.

Longarm motioned to the phony statue and asked, "When can I take it?"

"As soon as I have attached the gems to it," replied Dumont. "I must do that before the gold fully cools." He began working again, selecting suitable pieces of jewelry from the stuff Longarm had brought up to the room that morning and carefully mounting them on the statue.

Finding exact matches for the gems on the real thing was difficult, but when Dumont was finished, Longarm thought the end result looked close enough to pass muster. He hefted the fake Goddess and nodded in satisfaction. "Egan won't know it ain't real," he said. "Nickerson's another story. We don't know how much about the statue he's been told."

"We must hope for the best," Sir Harry said. "We have done all that is humanly possible."

"Except give them the real Goddess."

Sir Harry shook his head. "That is still out of the question."

"All right," Longarm said with a shrug. He held the statue out toward the Englishman. "Wrap this dingus up. I think I got just about enough time to get to Three Pines before sundown."

Chapter 13

Dumont took the statue from Longarm and turned to the table to wrap it in the same coverings that had shrouded the original. When he was finished, he handed it to Longarm and then wiped a sheen of sweat from his forehead. "Be very careful, Marshal," he said. "My lovely Alice's life depends on you."

"I have every confidence in you, Marshal," Sir Harry said. He slapped Longarm on the back with a pudgy hand. "I know you'll bring Alice back to us safe and sound."

Longarm hoped the Englishman was right. He put on his hat and went downstairs with the wrapped-up figurine tucked under his left arm.

Earlier in the day, he had returned the chestnut gelding to the livery stable. Now he went there again, and the hostler said, "Lemme guess, Marshal. You want a saddle horse."

Longarm grinned. "Right as rain, old son. Reckon you can fix me up?"

"Sure. If there's one thing I got plenty of, it's horses."

A few minutes later, Longarm was riding out of Virginia City on a golden sorrel stallion, a fine-looking animal. The false Golden Goddess was riding snugly in a saddlebag he had borrowed from the hostler. Longarm headed north on the Reno Road, following the line of the railroad's right-of-way just as he had done early in the pre-dawn hours of the morning.

He kept a close eye on his backtrail, but saw no sign of Hartley and Borden or anyone else following him. The sun slid closer and closer to the peaks of the mountain range to the west. Soon it would be touching them. Longarm didn't think Egan and Nickerson would kill Alice if he didn't show up exactly by sunset, but he didn't want to risk her life on that belief. He urged the sorrel on, heeling the animal into a ground-eating trot.

The road angled off to the northwest, away from the railroad tracks. Longarm kept the sorrel moving, and a short time later, he spotted Three Pines up ahead. He glanced at the mountains to the west. The sun still hovered above the peaks, but just barely.

Longarm's keen eyes searched for some sign of movement on top of the hill. The place seemed to be deserted. He knew better, though. His instincts told him that Egan and Nickerson and the other outlaws were up there right now, watching him as he rode closer. He left the trail and headed straight toward the hill.

As he drew closer, he reached down and opened the flap on the saddlebag. He took the paper-wrapped statue out of the pouch and held it over his head in plain sight. A moment later, as Longarm reached the bottom of the slope, several mounted figures appeared above, nudging their horses out from behind the trio of pine trees. Longarm rode on through the brush, then reined in to wait and see what was going to happen.

He searched among the riders for Alice, but didn't see her. Maybe the outlaws had decided not to give her to him, he thought bleakly. They might believe they could gun him down and take the statue anyway, without living up to their part of the bargain. What was bad, thought Longarm, was that that was probably right.

But if they tried, he would do his best to take some of

the polecats with him, especially Egan and Nickerson.

Then the group of horsemen parted a little, and Alice strode forward on foot, nudged on by a man mounted behind her. She walked out in front of the riders, definitely alive and seemingly all right.

Longarm heaved a sigh of relief, blowing out a breath he hadn't even been aware that he was holding. He lifted the statue over his head again and started the sorrel walking up the hill. Egan and Nickerson started down, flanking Alice as they had done that morning.

Egan reined in before the two parties met, also as he had done that morning. Nickerson followed suit as Egan called, "That's far enough, Mr. Lawman."

Longarm reined the sorrel to a halt. "How do you want to do this?" he asked.

Egan turned to Nickerson. "Go get the statue."

Nickerson hesitated and asked the same question that was burning in Longarm's mind. "What about the girl?"

"She stays here until you got the statue," rasped Egan. "Then when you start back up the hill, she starts down."

Nickerson didn't look too happy about being given orders like that, but he nodded anyway. "All right. That sounds like it'll work." He heeled his horse into motion.

Longarm watched tensely as the Chicago gunman rode slowly down the hill toward him. He didn't figure it would hurt anything if he planted the beginning of a wedge between Nickerson and Egan, so he said, "I thought you were the boss of this operation, Nickerson. Sir Harry said that Russian fella hired you to get the Golden Goddess, not Egan."

"As long as we get what we're after, I don't care who gives the orders," Nickerson said. He was only a few feet from Longarm now. He brought his mount to a stop and ordered, "Throw it over here."

Longarm hefted the statue in his hand. "You want me to just toss something this valuable?"

"Just give it here, damn it!" snapped Nickerson.

133

"All right," Longarm said. He sent the statue toward Nickerson with a soft toss.

Nickerson reached out to catch the small bundle, and as he did so, a sharp crack sounded behind Longarm and something passed through the air next to his ear with a flat *whap!* of sound. Nickerson's head jerked back, a black hole appearing just above his right eye. Bone fragments and gray matter exploded out the back of his head as the bullet punched a fist-sized exit wound in his skull. The statue hit the ground, and a second later so did Nickerson, every bit as dead as that paper-wrapped hunk of lead and gold.

"Shit!" howled Egan as he clawed at the butt of his right-hand gun. "It's an ambush!" The pearl-handled revolver came up and blasted a couple of shots toward Longarm.

Longarm wasn't there anymore. He had kicked his feet free of the stirrups and rolled out of the saddle as soon as he realized that somebody had shot Nickerson. He drew his Colt as he fell, but he was afraid to snap any shots toward Egan for fear of a stray bullet hitting Alice. Instead he scrambled for what little cover the mostly bare hillside provided, diving behind a small bump of rock. One of Egan's slugs tugged his hat off and sent it flying through the gathering twilight. Longarm noticed, somewhat irrelevantly, that the sun had dropped rapidly and had mostly disappeared behind the mountains to the west.

More gunfire crackled from the band of brush at the bottom of the hill. The bushwhackers must have concealed themselves there before either Longarm or the outlaws had arrived. Longarm had no idea who the hell they were, but at the moment he had other things to worry about, such as staying alive with all that lead whining around.

Most of the shots seemed to be directed toward the outlaws on the hilltop rather than him, but a few slugs thudded into the ground near him. The outcropping shielded him from the fire of Egan and the other outlaws, but he was in plain sight of the riflemen hidden below. Longarm threw a couple of shots toward the brush, then launched himself into a scrambling run toward a small gash in the hillside he had noticed off to his right. He stumbled as a slug burned across the front of his right thigh, ripping his trousers but not breaking the skin. He went forward in another rolling dive that carried him into the little gully, no doubt carved by a rivulet of water sometime in the past.

Longarm hunkered down as much as he could, making himself as small a target as possible. An occasional bullet whined off the rocks near him, but he sensed that the bushwhackers were just trying to keep him pinned down. They didn't really care whether they killed him or not. Longarm edged his head up, risking a glance at the hillside. He saw Nickerson's body still sprawled there. Nickerson's horse as well as Longarm's mount had spooked from all the shooting and trotted off in the other direction.

There was no sign of Egan or Alice.

Longarm's mouth quirked in a grimace under the sweeping longhorn mustache. Egan must have grabbed Alice and lit a shuck for the top of the hill. At least neither of them had been gunned down by the bushwhackers. That was a little consolation, Longarm thought.

But damned little. Alice was still in the hands of the outlaws, and Egan probably thought that Longarm was responsible for the ambush. As prone to rages as the outlaw was, he might kill Alice just to satisfy his need for revenge at being double-crossed.

Longarm didn't know who was down there in the brush. There were several riflemen, he was sure of that. The only possible suspects he could think of were the railroad detectives, Hartley and Borden. If they had trailed him out here to Three Pines that morning, as Longarm thought they might have, they could have figured out there was going to be an exchange of some sort here later on and hidden themselves and some hired guns in the brush to wait. The two railroad detectives were interested only in getting Egan. They didn't care about any kidnapping or ransom. The more Longarm thought about it, the more likely that theory seemed to him.

But if Hartley and Borden were leading the bushwhackers, why were they trying to kill *him*?

Longarm couldn't answer that one. He couldn't even be sure the railroad detectives were down there. All he could do was wait for the shooting to stop.

He heard the rolling thunder of hoofbeats from the other side of the hill. Egan and the rest of the gang were getting out while the getting was good.

Longarm risked another look out of the gully, only to jerk his head back quickly as a bullet knocked rock dust into his eyes. He heard more hoofbeats, closer this time. The bushwhackers must have had some horses hidden somewhere in the area, and they were pulling out too. Longarm stayed where he was, teeth gritted and jaw clenched in frustration, until all the sounds had died away and silence lay over the hillside like the shadows of twilight that had begun to fall. When he finally stuck his head up again, this time no shots came his way.

Standing up, Longarm lifted his Colt and held it ready just in case. The eerie silence continued. Egan and his men had made their getaway, and so had the bushwhackers. That left Longarm alone on the hillside with the dead Frank Nickerson. He walked toward the crumpled body of the Chicago gunman.

Nickerson was dead as a mackerel, all right. Longarm had known that. But as his eyes searched the rocky slope, he realized something else.

The Golden Goddess—the *fake* Golden Goddess—was gone.

Nickerson's horse had run off somewhere, but the sorrel Longarm had rented back in Virginia City was peacefully cropping grass beside the trail when Longarm trudged up a while later. The horse shied as he approached, but he was able to catch the reins and calm the animal down. At least he wouldn't have to walk all the way back to Virginia City, he thought grimly.

That was the only good thing that had come out of this

evening so far. Everything else had gone straight to hell in a hay wagon.

Alice was still in the hands of the outlaws, maybe wounded, maybe not, but definitely still a prisoner. The fake statue was gone, either grabbed up by Egan before he fled or snatched by one of the bushwhackers who had ventured out of the brush while the other riflemen covered him. That possibility seemed more likely to Longarm. Egan would have had to ride down the slope into the teeth of the gunfire to reach the statue, and Longarm didn't think he would have risked it.

Longarm swung up into the saddle and pointed the horse toward Virginia City. He wasn't sure what to do next, but Blackstreet and Dumont had to be informed of what had happened.

By the time he reached the settlement, full night had fallen, and Longarm wasn't any closer to figuring out exactly what had happened or what his next move should be. As he rode along C Street toward the Truckee Hotel, he looked for Hartley and Borden but didn't see them anywhere. He spotted Sheriff Reese striding along the boardwalk, making his evening rounds, but the local lawman just gave him the skunk-eye and moved on.

When Longarm reached the hotel, he saw that a fancy black carriage with a team of four magnificent black stallions attached to it was parked in front of the boardwalk. The carriage was decorated with elaborate silver flourishes, as was the harness on the team. Somebody who was mighty rich had just arrived in town.

Longarm frowned as he dismounted. He had no proof of it yet, but he had a sneaking suspicion he would find this wealthy newcomer in Sir Harry Blackstreet's suite.

The clerk at the desk gave Longarm's bullet-torn Stetson and trousers a curious glance as the big lawman strode through the lobby, but the man didn't try to stop him. Longarm clattered up the stairs and headed down the corridor toward Sir Harry's room. The door was jerked open before

Longarm got there, and the rotund Englishman looked out at him anxiously.

"I heard someone coming down the hall and hoped it was you, Marshal," Sir Harry said. "Where is Alice?"

"Egan still has her," Longarm replied grimly. He didn't stop walking, so Sir Harry was forced to step back and let him into the room. Longarm paused just across the threshold and looked around.

He saw immediately that his guess downstairs had been right. A stranger was sitting in one of the armchairs, his legs crossed casually, an expensive gray felt hat on his knee. The man was in late middle age, with a close-cropped beard that was mostly white, like his still-thick hair. His skin was tanned and weathered, and his dark eyes were deep-set under bushy brows. He wore a black suit and a silk vest, and his cravat was fastened with a stickpin decorated by what looked like a real diamond, and a good-sized one at that. Leaning against the arm of the chair was a black walking stick topped by a silver bear's head. The bear's mouth was open, as if it had been caught in mid-roar.

Two men stood behind the stranger, both of them burly and broad-shouldered and vaguely uncomfortable-looking in their town suits. Without hesitation, Longarm pegged them as bodyguards.

Off to one side at the table, Dumont stood, fidgeting nervously. "Alice?" he said, extending a hand tentatively. "My lovely Alice?"

Longarm just shook his head.

Dumont lifted his hands and tangled them in his hair. He slumped down into the chair by the table. "She cannot be dead!" he cried. "She cannot be!"

"I don't know if she's dead or alive," Longarm said bluntly. "All I know is that Egan rode off with her."

The stranger reached inside his coat and took out a long, thin, black cigar. In a deep, resonant voice, he said, "Sounds like you gents are having some trouble. Anything I can help you with?"

"Who the hell are you?" asked Longarm, knowing the man probably wasn't accustomed to being spoken to that way—but at the moment he didn't care.

The stranger seemed more amused than offended. "The name is Matthew Griffin," he said. He put the cigar in his mouth and continued around it, "You may have heard of me."

Longarm had heard of Matthew Griffin, all right. The man's name was usually mentioned in the same breath as Crocker, Stanford, Vanderbilt, and Morgan. He had interests in mines, railroads, steel mills, shipping, and anything else that could turn a profit. He had been one of the original Forty-Niners during the Gold Rush, Longarm recalled, and had just grown wealthier from there. Now Longarm was sure the fancy carriage downstairs belonged to Griffin.

Longarm looked at Sir Harry and inclined his head toward Griffin. "I reckon this is the fella who's supposed to buy the Golden Goddess from you?"

Sir Harry was sweating again. "That is correct. Mr. Griffin has made me a most generous offer for the figurine."

"What I set my mind on having, I usually get," Griffin said. He made a gesture, and one of the bodyguards struck a lucifer and lit the cigar for him. Griffin puffed on it for a second, then said, "I don't know what's going on here, Blackstreet, but I think it's time we conclude our arrangement. You *do* have the statue?"

Dumont shot to his feet and exclaimed, "No! You cannot give him the Goddess! Not while Alice is still being held captive by those horrible men!"

"Nickerson's not part of it anymore," Longarm said. "There was some shooting, and he wound up dead."

Sir Harry caught his breath as if he had just been punched hard in the ample belly. "Nickerson . . . is dead?" he said. "But . . . but how?"

"Some other bunch horned in and started slinging lead around," Longarm explained. He gestured toward his bullet-ventilated hat and the torn place on his trousers. "They almost winged me. But they got Nickerson right through the head just as we were making the switch. In the confusion, Egan got away with Alice."

"Gentlemen, I don't understand any of this," drawled Griffin. "All I know is, I came here to buy a statue from you, Blackstreet. Now, do you have it or not?"

Sir Harry swallowed hard. With Alice still in the hands of Egan, if he turned over the Golden Goddess to Griffin, he would lose the only real bargaining chip he had. When Egan cooled off and got over being livid over what he regarded as a double cross, he would probably try again to trade Alice for the statue.

But Griffin was becoming impatient. He clenched his teeth on the cigar and growled, "Damn it, what's it going to be? I either get my hands on that statue's dimpled little butt in the next five minutes, or I'm going back to San Francisco and taking my money with me!"

Sir Harry passed a shaking hand over his face. "I . . . I have no choice. Alice will understand. Yes, Mr. Griffin, I have the statue." He motioned weakly. "Dumont, hand me the Golden Goddess."

Dumont shook his head. "No. No, I cannot."

Sir Harry swung toward him angrily. "Damn your eyes, Dumont, do as I say! Give me the statue!"

Dumont let out a crazed laugh. He bent over and reached into the stew pot that was still sitting beside the table. His hand came out clutching the little statue. "You cannot have it!" he said as he began to back away. He lifted the figurine over his head.

"Dumont—!"

Longarm tensed, ready to lunge forward and grab Dumont. At the same time, Griffin made a gesture to his men that sent them forward, hands going under their coats for hidden guns.

"Take it then, if you must have it!" screeched Dumont, and moving with such speed that no one in the room had a chance to stop him, he brought the statue down and slammed it against the edge of the table, breaking it in half.

Sir Harry let out an incoherent shout. Griffin surged up

140

out of the chair with a curse. The magnate's men pulled their guns, but Longarm had his Colt out first. He leveled the revolver at them and snapped, "Hold it, boys! Drop those smoke poles."

Sir Harry stumbled toward Dumont, his hands out-stretched as if he intended to wrap his sausagelike fingers around the Frenchman's neck and choke the life out of him. He stopped short as Dumont continued laughing hysterically and brandished the broken piece of statue at him.

"Look!" Dumont cackled. "Look, you fools! Can you not see the truth?"

Longarm saw, all right, and his eyes grew wide with shock as he realized what he was seeing.

There was only a thin layer of gold on the piece of statue Dumont was holding. Under that gold was the dark gray of lead. Dumont had just busted open the false Golden Goddess, the duplicate over which he had labored so long and hard.

Which meant, thought Longarm, that the statue he had taken to the rendezvous with Egan and Nickerson at Three Pines had been the real thing. . . .

Chapter 14

A stunned silence hung over the room for a long moment before Dumont said, "I switched them! When you gave me the duplicate to wrap up, Marshal, I exchanged it for the real statue while neither of you were looking." The Frenchman threw back his head and laughed again. "You are all fools! Fools, I tell you!"

From the looks being directed at Dumont by Sir Harry, Griffin, and Griffin's two men, Longarm's gun was the only thing keeping them from beating the artist to death. Longarm kept his Colt trained on Griffin's men and said, "I told you boys to drop those guns."

Grudgingly, the hardcases leaned over and placed their pistols on the floor. "Kick 'em under the bed," Longarm ordered. The two men did so.

In a voice tight with anger, Griffin said, "Somebody had better tell me what's going on here and where the real statue is."

"It . . . it appears that an outlaw named Egan has it," Sir Harry said.

"Not necessarily," put in Longarm. "I told you, there was another bunch out there. I think it's a lot more likely they grabbed the statue during the fracas."

"Out where?" asked Griffin. "Damn it, I don't like being kept in the dark like this!"

Sir Harry took a deep breath. "My niece and traveling companion, Miss Alice Channing, was kidnapped by this desperado fellow called Egan, who was working with a criminal from Chicago named Nickerson. Nickerson was hired by a Russian expatriate in Constantinople to steal the Golden Goddess from me. He made several tries on the way here to Virginia City, but he was foiled each time. Finally, he and Egan joined forces and succeeded in capturing my niece, and they proposed to trade her for the statue. Dumont suggested that he make a duplicate of the Goddess so that Marshal Long could ransom. Alice with *that,* rather than the real thing." The Englishman glowered at Dumont. "Only, he switched the statues at the last moment, so the marshal was carrying the actual Golden Goddess when he went to meet Egan and Nickerson. Now do you understand?"

Griffin didn't say anything for several seconds. Then, with a snort of contempt, he said, "I understand you're trying to pull a fast one on me, Blackstreet. Who'd ever believe a load of hogwash like that story?"

"It's true, I swear it," Sir Harry said with desperation in his voice.

Stubbornly, Griffin shook his head. "Where's the real statue?"

"I tell you, I don't have it!" Panic was beginning to creep into Sir Harry's tone.

Griffin glanced at Longarm. "You're a lawman?"

"United States Deputy Marshal Custis Long."

"I want you to arrest this fat fraud of an Englishman," snapped Griffin. "He was going to try to pawn off a cheap imitation on me, instead of selling me the real thing as he agreed to."

"As far as I've seen, no money's changed hands," Longarm said, "so no law's been broken. And I ain't one of your hired hands, Griffin, so don't go ordering me around like I was."

With a visible effort, Griffin kept a tight rein on his temper. "I'm a citizen," he said slowly. "And I've got a right to press charges against Blackstreet. He tried to defraud me."

"Trying and doing ain't the same thing," Longarm pointed out. "Besides, he didn't know about the switch. That was Dumont's idea."

"You're sure about that?"

"Dumont fooled me too," Longarm said dryly. "Yeah, I'm sure."

"Thank you, Marshal," Sir Harry said.

Griffin put the cigar back in his mouth, puffed on it a couple of times, then said, "All right. I'll give you the benefit of the doubt, Blackstreet. But you'd better get that statue back. I didn't come all the way here from San Francisco for nothing."

Sir Harry glanced at Longarm and said almost pleadingly, "Marshal?"

"We'll get the statue back," Longarm said, although at the moment he had no idea where it was or who had it. But Alice was still in danger, and her life might still wind up depending on recovering the Golden Goddess.

"Twenty-four hours," Griffin said curtly. "That's all I'll give you. If I don't have the statue by then, I'll ruin you, Blackstreet. Maybe I can't see you behind bars, but I'll make you wish going to jail was the worst thing that ever happened to you."

Griffin put his hat on, gripped his walking stick tightly, and stalked toward the door. By the time he got there, one of his bodyguards had opened it and stepped out into the hall to make sure everything was safe for his employer. The other bodyguard slammed the door behind them.

Sir Harry sank down on the edge of the bed, looking as if he might pass out at any moment. "How?" he muttered. "How did everything go so wrong?" Then his gaze rose slowly to Dumont, and he had answered his own question.

Longarm moved between the two men, just in case Sir Harry got any ideas about strangling Dumont again. He said, "What's done is done. We've got to figure out what to do about it now."

"These men you say must have taken the statue . . . who were they?"

"I never got a look at them," replied Longarm. "I was too busy dodging bullets. But I've got an idea who they might be."

"Can you find them?"

"I can damn sure try." Longarm looked back and forth between Blackstreet and Dumont. "Can I leave you two here without having to worry about you killing each other?"

"I am an artist," Dumont said. "I am not a violent man."

"And I won't do any harm to the lunatic . . . yet," Sir Harry said.

"Good. Let's get Alice back safe and sound first, and then you two can settle anything you want to."

Sir Harry looked up at Longarm with a puzzled expression on his broad face. "But can you rescue Alice without finding the Golden Goddess?"

Longarm said, "I've got an idea about that too. . . ."

"Come on, mister, I'll show you a real good time," Juanita promised as she led the miner down the alley toward the shack where she conducted her business. "Make you feel real good." The alley was almost pitch black, but Juanita had made her way along it so many times over the past year she had been in Virginia City that she had no trouble finding her way in the dark.

The miner was very drunk, and Juanita hoped this wouldn't take long. There were several other men in the Alamo who would want to come back here with her later on, she thought. It was going to be a profitable night.

The man gripped her arm and pulled her to a stop. "How's about . . . a little sample first?" he asked thickly.

"No, we'll be there in just a minute," said Juanita, trying not to sound impatient. "You'll enjoy it, you'll see."

The miner's hand fumbled around and closed over her

left breast. He squeezed hard and slurred, "Jus' a lil' lovin' . . ."

Juanita tried to pull away from him. He was hurting her breast, and as he crowded her up against the wall of one of the buildings, he groped at her crotch with his other hand, trying to push up her long skirt. "Stop it!" she hissed. "Let go of me—"

She heard a thud, and suddenly the drunken miner sagged against her for a second before falling limply to the side. A tall, dark figure loomed in front of her in the alley, and a man's voice said, "That hombre was going to wake up in the morning with a headache anyway. Maybe it won't be too much worse for getting clouted."

"Thank you," Juanita gasped as she realized that this stranger had knocked the miner unconscious with a blow from the butt of his gun. The man was still holding the revolver. She could see the weapon only dimly, but she knew it was there, and she felt a faint tingle of fresh fear. Her "rescuer" might turn out to be worse than the drunken miner.

"Better not thank me yet, ma'am," Longarm said. "Not until you hear what it is I want you to do."

"Egan would kill me," Juanita said, stubbornly shaking her head. "I cannot do what you ask of me."

Longarm puffed on the cheroot in his mouth and said, "I don't see as you've got much choice."

"What will you do to me if I refuse?" Juanita asked disdainfully. "Have the sheriff put me in jail? I'm not afraid of going to jail."

"Maybe not, but you're afraid of Egan. If I have to hunt him up on my own, I'll make sure and let him know that you told me right where to find him."

Juanita's eyes widened with fear that bordered on terror. "You would not!"

Longarm said simply, "The hell I wouldn't."

That was a lie, of course, nothing but a bluff. Longarm didn't like threatening women, and he wasn't going to do anything that would send Egan gunning for the halfbreed whore. But if Juanita wanted to *think* he would, that was just fine.

The two of them were in Juanita's crib, a tiny, narrow room, little more than a lean-to on the back of a building. It was dimly lit by the flame of a guttering candle, but that was enough light for Longarm to see how torn Juanita was by the predicament in which he had put her. He had already figured out that she didn't feel any particular loyalty or emotional attachment to Egan; she was just scared of him and ambitious enough to want to keep on his good side. That was why she had ridden out the night before to warn him that Longarm was in Virginia City looking for him.

"There is nothing else I could do that would satisfy you?" asked Juanita as she reached up to toy with the knot that drew the neckline of her peasant blouse closed. Her fingers were deft as they unfastened the knot. Slowly, she drew the blouse down so that more and more of her breasts were revealed. The coral nipples that crowned each globe of creamy flesh popped into view.

Juanita was falling back on old habits, thought Longarm, trying to use her body to get what she wanted. It had surely worked for her many times in the past.

But not this time.

"You're a fine-looking woman, Miss Juanita," Longarm said, "and under other circumstances I reckon I'd enjoy getting to know you better, but right now I just don't have time. I need to know where Egan's hideout is."

Juanita leaned forward, her tongue darting out to lick enticingly over her lips. "I will do anything else you want, Marshal. *Anything*."

Longarm felt himself responding to her sensuous presence. His manhood began to harden. Juanita must have seen that, because she stepped closer and reached down to rub his hardness through the front of his trousers.

"I can show you things you have never experienced before," she promised.

Longarm doubted that mighty seriously. For one thing,

he was nearly twice as old as this gal and had known what men and women did with each other for longer than she'd been alive. He reached up and took the cheroot out of his mouth, then used his other hand to cup her chin and tilt her head back. His mouth came down on hers in a hard, hungry kiss. Her body pressed against his, and her still-bare breasts flattened against his chest.

But when he took his lips away from hers, he said, "I still got to know where to find Egan."

The hand that had been caressing him flashed up and streaked toward his face as she spat a curse at him. With a move that seemed almost lazy, he caught her wrist before she could strike him.

"If I have to find Egan on my own, you'd damned well better hope that I kill him," grated Longarm. "Otherwise, he's going to come looking for you."

"Bastard!" Juanita said between clenched teeth.

Longarm just shrugged.

He saw the fight go out of her then. Her head drooped. She took a step back from him, and he let go of her wrist. She pulled her blouse up and retied it. Without looking at him, she said in a dull voice, "I will tell you where to find him."

"Nope," said Longarm. "You'll *show* me."

Juanita's head jerked up again. "Show you?" she repeated.

"That's right. Otherwise you're liable to send me riding into some sort of trap. We're leaving here and riding straight to wherever it is Egan's holed up, so you won't have a chance to tip anybody off."

Juanita shook her head and said, "I cannot."

Longarm sighed. "We're back to that again, are we?"

"No, I mean it. I cannot. I can take you to the pass in the mountains where I always met him, but from there I was blindfolded each time he took me to his camp."

"Blindfolded?" Longarm didn't know whether to believe her or not.

"Yes. Egan never trusted me." A bitter edge crept into

148

her voice as she added, "He only used me for his pleasure."

Longarm rubbed his jaw. He had hoped he could pressure Juanita into revealing where Egan's hideout was located so that he could sneak into the place and try to rescue Alice. Then he would deal with figuring out the current whereabouts of the Golden Goddess. But if Juanita didn't know how to get there, he was back to making a blind search in the vicinity of the pass where he had trailed her the night before.

"I want you to think about it," Longarm said grimly. "Even if you were blindfolded, you must remember something about it. What sort of trail did the horse go over? Were there any unusual sounds? Anything like that?"

Juanita frowned for a moment, then said, "The trail was steep and rough, I know that. But most trails in the mountains are steep and rough. I remember hearing something, though, just before we reached Egan's camp. A roaring sound."

"Like a waterfall?" suggested Longarm. That was the only thing he could think of that would make a roaring sound in the mountains.

Juanita nodded eagerly. "Yes, just like a waterfall. And I remember now, I felt the touch of something wet on my face, like spray from where a stream falls into a pool."

"Anything else?"

The soiled dove caught her lower lip between her teeth and chewed on it as she thought. Finally, she shook her head. "No. That is all."

Longarm's cheroot had gone out. He put it back in his mouth anyway and clamped his teeth on it. "That's better than nothing," he said. "Much obliged."

Juanita sighed in relief. "Now I do not have to come with you?"

Longarm considered and said, "Nope."

"Good."

"But I still don't reckon I can trust you not to try to warn Egan."

Moving too fast for her to stop him, he brought up a

loosely balled fist and clipped her on the jaw with it. The punch rocked her head back, and her eyes rolled up in their sockets. As she sagged loosely toward the floor, Longarm caught her and lowered her as gently as possible onto her narrow bunk. Then, while she was still stunned, he tore strips of fabric from the bottom of her long skirt and bound her wrists and ankles tightly enough so that it would take her a while to work loose, but not so tight as to do any real damage to her. He followed that by gagging her with another piece of cloth.

By the time Juanita could free herself, he would be well on his way to the vicinity of Egan's hideout, Longarm thought. By then it wouldn't matter what she did.

But he still felt bad enough about knocking her out and tying her up to tuck a five-dollar gold piece into the pocket of her skirt before he left.

The hostler at the livery stable was getting used to this. As soon as he saw Longarm coming, he went to saddle a fresh horse.

This one was a hammer-headed, mouse-colored dun with a dark stripe down its back and a mean look in its eyes. "He's a better horse than what he looks like," the holster said. "Just mind that you keep an eye on him. He likes to take a nip out of people's hides when they're not watching."

"I'll remember that," Longarm said dryly. He mounted up and rode out of the barn.

He was glad he had a knack for directions and landmarks, he thought as he skirted the base of Mount Davidson and headed deeper into the mountains. Otherwise, it would be easy to get lost wandering around up there in the dark. As it was, he was worried about finding the canyon Juanita had followed to the pass the night before. An hour passed while Longarm rode by starlight. The moon hadn't risen yet.

By the time it did, he had found the pass and was carefully making his way along it. The silvery glow from the moon showed him the slash of darkness between two beetling bluffs that marked the pass. He dismounted and went through it on foot, leading the dun and being careful not to make too much noise. He didn't know how close Egan's hideout was, but it was near enough so that a guard posted there had seen Juanita's signal with the match the previous night.

Longarm paused at the far end of the pass and listened intently. He hoped he could hear the sound of the waterfall Juanita had described, but nothing like that came to his ears. The only noises he heard were the distant screech of an owl and some rustling in the brush near the pass caused by a small animal.

A natural trail, probably made by deer and other animals, led away from the pass. Longarm followed it, still leading the dun. It wound down a steep slope into a valley that was floored with grass. Longarm paused again, and this time he heard something—the trickle of a stream.

Where there was a waterfall, there had to be a stream feeding it, Longarm reasoned. A few minutes later, when he found the narrow creek that meandered along the edge of the valley, he asked himself whether the waterfall was upstream or down from there. There was no way of knowing. His instincts prodded him to go upstream, so that was the way he went.

A few minutes later, the valley ended at a solid rock wall. Longarm muttered a curse under his breath. The stream he had been following emerged seemingly from the cliff, but he knew it was flowing from an underground passage. He had picked the wrong direction.

Or had he? He paused and listened again, and he thought he heard a faint roaring sound coming from the direction he had been going. Unwilling to give up, he began following the line of the cliff, and after about ten minutes, he came to a narrow trail that angled up the face of the rock. It was wide enough for one rider, but that was all.

Longarm thought about leaving the dun, but then he started up the ledge, leading the horse behind him. The cliff bulged out, overhanging the trail so that Longarm had to stoop slightly to clear the rock. Then the trail turned and the cliff receded so that he could stand up again. He followed the ledge as it climbed steadily around a long, gentle curve.

The trail reached level ground, and Longarm found himself on a long, wide bench that thrust out from yet another cliff in the distance. The sound of the waterfall was louder now, and he felt a surge of excitement as he spotted moonlight reflecting off a column of water that tumbled down the perpendicular cliff. This was the spot; he knew it. Somewhere on this bench the stream went underground only to emerge down below from the cliff he had just climbed.

The waterfall was about a quarter of a mile away. Longarm started toward it, still leading the dun. He paused long enough to slide his Winchester from the saddle boot and make sure there was a round in the chamber. Then he went forward again, walking as quietly as possible. He didn't stop until he caught a faint whiff of wood smoke in the air.

That smoke had to come from a campfire. He was close now, close enough so that it was probably a good idea to leave the horse behind. Otherwise, the dun might scent the horses belonging to Egan's gang and let out a whinny. Longarm tied the reins to an aspen sapling and cat-footed on, following the smoke now as well as the sound of the waterfall.

Less than five minutes later, he saw the orange glow of a fire. It was set back in a hollow in the cliff face, about fifty yards beyond the pool formed by the waterfall and shielded from sight of it by a bulge in the cliff face. That was why Juanita had heard the waterfall but not seen it.

Longarm crouched in some brush to study the situation. He twisted his head and looked back across the valley. He could see the pass where Juanita had signaled to the gang. It was only about five hundred yards away, though he estimated he had traveled at least two miles to reach this spot. Harp Egan had picked a good place for his hideout. With the high cliff behind it, no one could attack from that direction, and the pass was the only entrance into the valley that ultimately led here. A couple of good marksmen with rifles could cover the pass and keep anyone from coming through it.

Longarm hunkered on his heels. As he watched the camp, he saw men moving around the fire, and then he caught a glimpse of fair hair. His eyes narrowed. He wished he had a pair of field glasses. That had to be Alice he had seen. He watched intently.

A tall, broad-shouldered man—Egan, more than likely—walked around the fire with something in his hand. He offered it to another figure on the far side of the fire, and as that person looked up, Longarm saw the fair hair again. He was sure now—that was Alice. She was alive.

She shook her head, and Egan shrugged and turned away. He had just offered her something to eat, Longarm realized, and she had turned it down. Too proud to take an outlaw's grub. Longarm hoped she hadn't been starving herself ever since Egan had kidnapped her. If she had, she was probably pretty weak, and that could hold them back while the two of them were trying to get away.

In the darkness, Longarm's mouth curved in a sardonic smile. Here he was, thinking about their getaway . . . when first of all he had to figure a way to get Alice the hell out of there.

Chapter 15

Carefully, Longarm counted the men he could see either moving around the camp or squatting next to the fire. There were seven of them, including Egan, and a couple of blanket-wrapped shapes that could be sleeping men. Longarm was sure there was at least one man standing guard somewhere in the darkness. That meant eight to ten outlaws, and quite possibly another one or two. Not very good odds, he decided.

So he would have to try to whittle them down a mite, he thought with a rather bleak grin.

Longarm's gaze lifted to the face of the cliff. It had been scored and weathered by the passage of centuries, and he was fairly certain he could climb it if he had to. He didn't see what good that would do right now, however.

Then his eyes narrowed as he spotted shadows on the wall formed by bulges of rock. In the bright moonlight, he could tell that some of those bulges were separate chunks of stone that were perched precariously on narrow ledges. He looked at the base of the cliff and saw large pieces of rock scattered around in several places. That told him those boulders fell from time to time, busting into smaller pieces when they hit the ground. Egan and the other outlaws had to be aware of that danger, but under the overhang where their camp was located, they would be safe from any plummeting rocks.

Longarm decided the thing to do was lure them out into the open.

He slipped back to the dun and reached into the saddlebag for the box of .44 cartridges he had brought with him. Then he moved up into the brush again, stopping when he was still fifty yards from the camp. He cleared a spot on the ground and took a handful of cartridges from the box. Using his teeth for leverage, he twisted the lead bullets out of the cartridges and poured the gunpowder from each of them onto the ground, making a small mound of the stuff. He took a dozen more cartridges and placed them on the mound, turning them so that their bases were firmly seated in the mound of gunpowder. Then he opened more cartridges and began making a narrow trail of the powder from them, stretching it out as far as he could. Once this makeshift fuse was burning, the brush around it would conceal the glow of sparks from the camp unless one of the outlaws happened to be looking directly at it.

When he was satisfied, Longarm nodded grimly to himself and stowed away in his coat pocket the cartridges that were left. Then, holding the Winchester firmly in his left hand, he used his right to fish a lucifer out of his vest pocket. Snapping it to life on an iron-hard thumbnail, he held the flame to the end of the gunpowder trail and saw the stuff catch with a sputter of sparks. He backed away quickly and then turned and moved through the brush in a crouching run.

He had gone several yards when the sparks reached the mound of gunpowder and set it off with a whoosh. The heat of the little explosion started a small fire in the brush, and more importantly, also ignited several of the cartridges Longarm had left there. They went off with a ragged staccato of whip-cracks, and Longarm heard yells of alarm from the outlaw camp.

More of the bullets blasted as the fire heated them, and

it sounded for all the world like the hideout was under attack by several men. Egan's gang must have thought so, because the owlhoots all grabbed iron and came running out to defend the place. Longarm was tempted to take potshots at a few of them, since he could see them so well in the moonlight, but instead he directed his bullets at strategic spots on the cliff face, firing the Winchester as fast as he could pull the trigger and lever another round into the chamber.

The slugs slammed into the rock just below some of the boulders perched there, and just as Longarm had hoped, the rocks were jarred into falling. They tumbled down, some of them striking the cliff face and bouncing, others falling straight to the bench. The ones that hit the cliff started more rocks falling.

Longarm knew his shots would draw the fire of the outlaws. He flung himself aside as the desperadoes opened up in his direction. Bullets whipped through the brush above him as he hugged the ground and listened to the rumbling sound that welled up as the rocks fell. He heard crashes as they struck the ground, and men started to yell and scream. The shooting stopped.

Longarm risked a glance and saw that clouds of dust from the avalanche filled the air. He surged to his feet and started running toward the camp, the Winchester held ready in his hands. No one fired at him. As he plunged into the billowing dust, a figure loomed up in front of him. Longarm had time to see that it was one of the outlaws before the man cursed and tried to swing a gun toward him. Longarm drove the butt of the Winchester into the man's face and felt bone crunch under the blow. The outlaw went over backward.

Longarm kept moving, trying not to cough as the dust stung his eyes and nose and throat. The rumbling died away, which meant the rocks had stopped falling. The outlaws, at least the ones who hadn't been crushed or otherwise incapacitated by the falling rocks, would still be stunned and disoriented for a few minutes. They wouldn't have any idea how many enemies they were facing. Longarm had to take advantage of that.

He hoped he was still going in the right direction. It would be easy to get turned around in the shadows and dust. The wall of the cliff appeared in front of him. He stopped in time to keep from running into it. Obviously, he had missed the overhang where the camp was located, but was it to the right or the left?

Longarm took a chance on the right and saw almost immediately that he had guessed correctly. The cliff face fell away, and the big lawman almost stumbled into the campfire, which was still burning. Alice Channing, who was on her feet now, shrank back from him and screamed. He must have scared her, coming out of the cloud of dust like that.

Before he could tell her who he was, a gun blasted to his right. Longarm saw the muzzle flash from the corner of his eye. He pivoted in that direction and fired the Winchester from the hip. The slug drove into the chest of the outlaw who was running toward him and flung the man backward.

"Alice, it's me, Custis Long!" said Longarm as he grabbed Alice's arm. "Let's go!" He wheeled away from the campfire, hauling her along with him.

More shots rang out. Longarm heard bullets ricocheting from the cliff. Egan's men were firing blindly now, and they'd be lucky if they didn't ventilate each other. That would be all right with him, thought Longarm. He stayed close to the cliff and pulled Alice along with him.

He would have to hope that the dun could find its way back to Virginia City on its own, because they damned sure couldn't go back for the horse. They went the other way instead. If they had tried to escape down the narrow trail into the valley, the outlaws would have been able to pick them off, and if by some miracle they avoided being killed there, the trail up the far side of the valley to the pass would be just as dangerous. Better to go where no one would expect them to go, Longarm thought.

In this case, up.

When they had followed the bench several hundred yards, sticking close to the base of the cliff the whole way, Longarm stopped and looked back. He didn't see any signs of pursuit. The dust had settled around the outlaw camp. He heard hoofbeats rattling on stone and knew some of the men were riding down the trail toward the valley, looking for him. A couple more stood around the campfire, holding rifles. Longarm hoped only a handful of the outlaws were still alive. He hoped that Harp Egan wasn't one of them.

Satisfied that they weren't in any immediate danger, Longarm took the time to pull Alice into his arms for a hug. She was trembling, and Longarm used his free hand to stroke her hair. "Are you all right?" he asked in a whisper.

Her face was buried against his chest. He felt her nod. "Y-yes," she managed to say, shakily. "They . . . they didn't harm me. Some of the men wanted to . . . to have their way with me . . . but that man Nickerson wouldn't let them, and then after he was killed, neither would Egan."

"Well, we've got that to be grateful for anyway." Longarm stepped back a little and cupped her chin. "Can you climb?"

"Climb?" repeated Alice.

Longarm pointed up the cliff face with a thumb.

Alice turned her head to look up, and she gasped, "No . . . no, I couldn't possibly . . ."

"It's the only way out of here," Longarm told her. "Just take it slow and easy. The face isn't near as sheer and smooth as it looks from down here. I'll stay here at the bottom to cover you in case they decide to look in this direction." *Once they've figured out we didn't head for the valley,* he thought but didn't add out loud.

"I just can't—" Alice began.

"Sure you can," Longarm cut in. He pulled his Colt from its holster on the cross-draw rig and pressed it into her hand. "Here, take this and stow it somewhere. Once you get to the top, you're going to cover me while I'm climbing up."

"I . . . I've never fired a gun."

"And I hope you don't have to tonight," Longarm said sincerely. "But if you do, just point the barrel at the outlaws and pull the trigger. It's a double-action, so you don't have to cock the hammer first. You may have to pull pretty hard, though, since you're not used to it and I don't like a hair trigger." He didn't really expect her to hit anything if she had to shoot, but maybe she could make enough noise to keep the outlaws distracted while he climbed, if it came to that.

Alice nodded. "All right. I . . . I'll try."

"Good girl. Now, go on. Get to climbing."

She opened the front of her dress and placed the gun inside it. There was a risk in carrying a weapon like that, but some risks had to be taken. Despite his reassuring words to her, Longarm knew the climb wouldn't be easy either. But Alice reached up, found a handhold, lifted her foot, wedged it against a small outcropping of rock, and started to climb.

Longarm wished he could have made the ascent with her so that he could help her, but if they were both on the cliff face at the same time, they would be easy targets if Egan's men happened to come along. By now, the outlaws who had ridden down to the valley would be starting to wonder why they hadn't caught up to whoever had attacked the hideout. The ones who were still by the campfire had to know that Alice was gone, and they would surely come looking for her, likely thinking that she had just run off during the confusion. The two of them didn't have much time, Longarm knew.

He tilted his head back and looked up. Alice was about fifteen feet above him, moving slowly and selecting her handholds and footholds with care before committing her weight to them. Longarm felt himself being torn, a part of him wanting her to hurry, while another part knew she had to take it slow and easy or risk falling. He knew he would experience the same mixed emotions when he himself started the climb.

His eyes went back and forth from the cliff to the hide-out. There was still no sign that the outlaws were coming this way.

A sudden rustling of grass was the only warning he had that someone was rushing at him from behind. He turned and dropped at the same time. The man lunging at him was swinging a rifle like a club, and the weapon's stock whipped over Longarm's head to strike the cliff face instead. It shattered against the rock, and the man cried out in pain as the impact shivered up the barrel of the rifle into his hands.

Longarm didn't want this fight to produce any more sounds than it had to. He jabbed with the Winchester, thrusting its barrel into the belly of the outlaw. The man's breath whooshed out as he doubled over. Longarm stepped closer and struck with the rifle again, clipping the man on the temple with the butt. The outlaw fell in an unconscious heap at Longarm's feet.

Longarm drew a deep breath and blew it out slowly. That had been a close one. The man who had jumped him must have been the guard, who had been posted away from the camp and hadn't been caught in the avalanche. Longarm wondered if there were any other sentries roaming around. This one could have done for him if he'd just gunned him down instead of trying to take him alive.

Longarm looked up. The cliff was between eighty and a hundred feet tall, he estimated, and Alice was halfway to the top by now. She was still climbing steadily. She was handling this in a cooler fashion that he had anticipated.

A shout drew Longarm's attention. He looked toward the camp and saw men on horseback riding in. At least some of the outlaws who had gone down to the valley had returned to report no luck in finding whoever had attacked the hideout. Longarm could hear the time left to him ticking away as surely as if he'd held his watch pressed to his ear.

Alice was moving faster now, he saw when he checked again. The slope wasn't as steep as she neared the top of the cliff. She was three-fourths of the way up. Longarm

160

wished he could have waited until she was all the way to the top, but he sensed that he had pushed this as long as he could. He started climbing, his progress made more awkward by the fact that he had to carry the Winchester too. He wished it had a sling on it so he could have put it over his shoulder.

He had climbed a lot more cliffs in his life than a well-bred young Englishwoman like Alice. He moved quicker than she did, sensing instinctively which grips would hold him and which would not. The ground began to fall away underneath him.

When he had climbed about twenty feet, he paused and leaned back slightly so that he could peer up the cliff above him. He could no longer see Alice, probably because of the way the cliff face angled in toward the top. At least, he hoped that was the reason. He knew she hadn't fallen. He couldn't have missed that. Hugging the cliff again, he resumed the climb.

The halfway point came quickly. Longarm felt a slight easing in his muscles as the slope became not quite so steep. Now he could see all the way to the top of the cliff, and Alice was nowhere in sight. Then, abruptly, her head popped into view as she stuck it out and looked down toward him. She waved the hand in which she clutched the Colt revolver.

Longarm grinned. He pulled himself up another five feet, then five more and five more. Less than forty feet to the top now. He shifted his handhold, dug the toe of his right boot into a good-sized crack in the rock, and heaved up—

"Up there!"

The shout came from below. Longarm bit back a curse. He recognized the gravelly voice and knew that Egan was still alive. He had been hoping that a particularly large rock had fallen on the boss outlaw and turned him into something resembling strawberry preserves.

There was nothing he could do except keep climbing. He couldn't turn and fire the Winchester down at the outlaws.

161

The rifle's recoil would probably knock him right off the cliff if he tried.

A shot blasted, and a slug smashed into the rock off to Longarm's left. Shooting upwards like that was tricky, but he was sure the owlhoots would get the range sooner or later, probably sooner. He practically lunged up another couple of feet, his hands slipping a little before they found a secure purchase. The Winchester, which was tucked under his arm, almost slipped out. He clamped his elbow against his side to hold the rifle in place. He might need it later.

If he made it to the top of the cliff alive.

Suddenly, a gun cracked above him. Alice was firing down at the outlaws. To Longarm's surprise, he heard one of them yelp in pain. Alice had actually hit something through blind luck. She fired again, and the muzzle flash told Longarm she had moved off to the right, so that she would have a better angle and wouldn't have to fire too closely past him.

He scrambled upward, taking even more chances now, as Alice emptied all five shots in the revolver. Longarm wished he had thought to thumb a cartridge into the empty chamber that he habitually kept under the hammer, but that hadn't occurred to him. Not that one more shot would have made a hell of a lot of difference, he told himself. He was only about ten feet from the rim now.

The outlaws had stopped shooting while Alice was blazing away at them. Now their fire resumed, and Longarm felt bullets tug at the leg of his trousers and the sleeve of his coat. When a rock came loose under his hand, he tossed it down, hoping it would land on somebody's head. His legs pushed hard, thrusting him toward the top of the cliff.

More slugs whined past him, but now the gunmen were missing behind him. The angle of the cliff caused that, he realized. As long as they were gathered at the base of the cliff, they no longer had a clear shot at him. But it wouldn't take them long to figure that out too.

His hand closed over the rimrock. He pulled himself up, kicking hard with his feet, and rolled over the edge of the cliff. He wasn't sure what he would find there, but almost anything would be better than hanging out there on the cliff like a sitting duck.

He and Alice were on a narrow ridge that fell away into another valley, Longarm saw as he sat up and looked around. Alice crawled toward him, keeping low so that the outlaws couldn't see her from below. As she came up to him, she asked anxiously, "Are you all right, Marshal?"

He took the empty Colt from her and jammed it back in its holster. "I'm fine," he said, "but we got to get out of here." He pointed along the ridge toward the spot where it curved around and joined the shoulder of a mountain. "Follow this ridge that direction. I'll be coming along behind you."

"What are you going to do?"

"Try to discourage Egan and his boys from following us," Longarm said.

On his knees, he moved closer to the brink and thrust the barrel of the Winchester over. He fired down, swinging the weapon in a fanlike motion that would spread the bullets out. That probably made a few of the outlaws hop, he thought as he rolled away from the edge and reached for the box of cartridges in his pocket, and it would sure make them think twice about trying to climb up the cliff after the fugitives. The outlaws still couldn't be sure how many men were up here and whether or not Alice had escaped up the cliff too.

Quickly, Longarm reloaded the rifle. He came up into a crouch and ran after Alice, who was hurrying along the ridge, staying down low enough on the slope so that she couldn't be seen. Longarm didn't shoot anymore. He knew he could count on the outlaws lying low for several minutes anyway, as they gathered their courage and tried to decide if it was safe to attempt to climb the cliff.

Longarm grinned. Luck had been with him and Alice, no question about that. But luck tended to follow an hombre who didn't mind taking a chance now and then, at least for a while. His would run out someday, he thought—but it hadn't yet.

He caught up with Alice. She looked over her shoulder at him and asked, "Are they chasing us?"

"Not yet," Longarm told her.

She was gasping for breath. "How are we . . . going to get back . . . to Virginia City?"

Longarm hadn't quite worked that out yet. Right now, he just wanted to put as much distance as possible between them and Egan's bunch. Then, when they couldn't go any farther, they would hunt someplace they could hole up for the rest of the night.

Come morning— if they were still alive—he'd figure out what to do next.

Chapter 16

The rays of the rising sun slanting in through the narrow opening at the mouth of the cave woke Longarm. For a moment, he didn't stir except to open his eyes and move his head a little so that the sun wouldn't be blinding him. He blinked a couple of times. He was a mite disgusted with himself, because he hadn't meant to go to sleep when he and Alice had crawled in here the night before. Exhaustion had finally claimed him, though, and he figured he must have dozed off a couple of hours earlier.

After everything that had happened, it was a little hard to believe that he was still alive, let alone that he was lying here with a beautiful woman snuggled in his arms. Alice had her head pillowed on his shoulder, and his left arm was partially numb because of it. Longarm shifted a little, trying to relieve the pressure on his arm without waking Alice. She murmured a protest and wiggled around some without opening her eyes. As she settled down again, her head on Longarm's chest this time, her breathing became deep and regular and he knew she was still asleep. He was able to lift his left hand and shake it lightly so that it prickled with pins and needles as the blood began to flow freely again.

Longarm twisted his head to look around. The cave in

which he and Alice had hidden had a rock floor with only a thin layer of dirt on it. But something—a bear, more than likely—had dragged some pine branches in here and pounded them down to make a sort of bed. The varmint probably denned up and hibernated in here during the winter, thought Longarm. At any rate, the branches and the dead needles were better than lying on rock and dirt.

The cave was only about six feet wide; Longarm knew he couldn't have stretched out sideways across it without having to bend his legs. It tapered down toward the front into an even narrower opening. He'd had to turn to squeeze through it the night before after sticking his arm inside and scratching a lucifer to life against the rough wall so he could take a gander around. Even with Harp Egan and the other outlaws on their trail, Longarm hadn't been willing to crawl into a strange cave without making sure he and Alice were going to be its only occupants.

The cave had been empty. In the glow of the match, Longarm had been able to see the far end, a dozen or so feet away. The ceiling was low, just tall enough for him to stand up without hitting his head. The place probably seemed roomier to Alice, since she was considerably smaller than he was.

The two of them were still alone this morning, Longarm saw as he looked around. The Winchester lay on the floor of the cave beside them, close at hand. But he hadn't needed it, since no one had found them there. While making their way around the mountain the night before, Longarm had tried to stick to the rockiest ground he could find so that they wouldn't leave tracks. It looked like he had succeeded, because Egan hadn't been able to trail them there.

Unless the boss outlaw was waiting outside for them.

Longarm listened intently, heard nothing except the chattering of blue jays and other birds. Nobody was around or the birds wouldn't have been making such a racket. He smiled. He and Alice were safe for the time being.

One of her legs was thrown across his hips. She shifted

again in her sleep, scooting over so that she was lying pretty much on top of him. Her breath was warm against his throat. He became aware of the way her breasts were flattened against his chest and her stomach was molded against his groin. The thought of all that soft female flesh so close by made his shaft start to grow and harden.

A moment later, Alice's hips moved. She hitched herself up higher so that her pelvis ground over his now-erect manhood. Longarm bit back a groan as her hips worked slowly back and forth, dry-humping him through their clothes. The little minx had to be awake, he thought. Surely she wasn't tormenting him like this in her sleep.

But her breathing was as steady as ever, if a little quicker now. Her hands were resting on his shoulders. The fingers flexed slightly, digging in and gripping as she began to move her hips even faster. Longarm craned his neck so that he could see her face. Alice's eyes were closed, but her lips were parted and her breaths began coming through them in little pants of desire.

He wondered what the hell, if anything, she was dreaming right now. He was going to feel mighty damned foolish if she called out some other man's name.

"Custis!" cried Alice. "Oh, Custis!"

That made Longarm feel considerably better. He put his arms around her as her hips began thrusting so hard at his groin that they came up completely off him each time before lunging down again. After a moment of that, she suddenly stiffened for a few seconds, and then a huge shudder went through her.

Longarm couldn't recollect ever making a woman come in her sleep before, and just by holding her at that.

Alice's head popped up, her short blond hair tousled prettily around her face. Her eyes were wide open. "Oh!" she gasped. "Marshal Long!" Color began to flood redly into her cheeks. "I . . . I'm so sorry! I never meant to . . . to—"

"It's all right," Longarm told her quietly. "I'm mighty glad you did."

She looked at him for a moment, then leaned her head forward and kissed him, a soft meeting of lips that quickly grew harder and more passionate. Longarm's shaft was still hard as a steel bar, and Alice had to feel it digging into her belly. She proved it by the way her hips began to glide back and forth again.

She lifted her head, breaking the kiss to ask, "Is everything . . . all right?"

"Listen to the birds," said Longarm. "There's nobody around here but us."

Alice put her hands on his chest and pushed herself into a sitting position, still straddling his hips. "Then we need to get rid of these clothes," she said as her hands went to the buttons of her dress.

Longarm couldn't have agreed more.

He watched in appreciation as Alice unfastened the buttons and spread the dress open. Under it she wore a thin shift through which her dark, erect nipples were plainly visible. She pulled the dress off her shoulders and slipped her arms out of the sleeves, then reached down to the hem at the bottom and gathered it up before lifting her hips briefly to pull the garment up and over her head. That left her in only the shift, stockings, and her shoes. The shift was shorter and easier to peel off, and once it was gone she was perched atop Longarm mostly nude.

"Now for you," she breathed. She bent forward and went to work on his buttons.

Longarm enjoyed the view while Alice was doing that. Her breasts hung there enticingly, only a short distance from his face. He could see the faintly visible tracery of blue veins under the surface of creamy flesh.

When she had his vest and shirt unbuttoned, she slid back so that she was sitting on his thighs. That allowed him to sit up and take off the coat, vest, and shirt. Then, as he reclined again after dropping the clothes under his back to form a mattress of sorts on the bed of pine branches, Alice unbuttoned his trousers and opened them, then pulled them down along with his underwear. She made a sound of approval in her throat as the long, thick, heavy pole of male flesh sprang free from its confinement and stood up tall and proud. After a little more shifting around, Longarm's trousers were down around his ankles.

Alice turned so that she was facing away from Longarm. He had a pretty good idea what she had in mind as she knelt over him and then leaned down so that she could take the head of his manhood in her mouth. From this angle, with her knees spread and planted on either side of his chest, he had a perfect view of the inviting opening between her legs and the fine blond down that surrounded it. He could even see the puckered brown ring that was above it from this angle, set in the valley between the perfect round cheeks of her rump.

Longarm used his thumbs to open the gates of her femininity and lifted his head so that he could reach her with his tongue. As he began running it along the already moist portal, Alice moaned and closed her lips even tighter around his shaft. One of her hands reached between his legs and cupped his balls.

Longarm's tongue probed as deeply into her femaleness as it could for a moment. Then he began licking and sucking and biting gently at the folds of flesh. The middle finger of his right hand strayed upward and penetrated her other opening, exploring the extremely tight, buttery softness inside. Alice's mouth opened around his shaft as she let out a groan of pure pleasure. Then she started sucking him again with renewed vigor, swallowing even more of his manhood.

He didn't mind bringing her to another climax this way, but he didn't want to spend his seed in her mouth. So after another wave of shudders went through her, causing her to clench her thighs against his rib cage and bear down hard on the finger he had inside her, he pulled back. Even as overwhelmed as she must have been by the sensations cascading through her, Alice seemed to sense what he wanted, because she let go of his shaft and turned around, positioning herself over his pole. The head of it glistened from a mixture of her saliva and its own natural juices.

Alice lowered herself onto him, and she was so wet that he slipped inside her immediately. She slid all the way down, so that he felt the end of his shaft bumping against the back of her heated chamber. Both of them were too worked up to put off the culmination they both needed and wanted so desperately. Longarm grabbed Alice's hips and held her in place as his hips surged up off the ground. He wouldn't have believed it possible, but he buried his manhood just a little deeper inside her by doing so. He felt his seed boiling up.

It erupted in a series of white-hot blasts, filling Alice. She cried out incoherently as Longarm spurted inside her. His climax seemed to go on forever, spasm after spasm. He gritted his teeth to keep from yelling at the sheer ecstasy of it.

Finally, he had emptied himself, and his head sagged back onto his bunched-up clothes. Alice fell forward onto his chest, every muscle in her body limp. Longarm folded his arms around her and held her tightly as both of them breathed heavily.

A few minutes rolled past as they lay there, still awash in sensation, unaware of anything except each other. One of Longarm's hands swooped down Alice's back in a caress, then slid up the curve of her rump to cup the cheek on that side. He felt the deep dimple under his palm and then explored it with the tip of his index finger. Alice giggled.

"That tickles," she said. "That dimple has always been one of my most sensitive spots."

"Well, then . . ." Longarm began with a grin. Then he stopped short as he realized that the birds were no longer singing. They might have been frightened off by the cries of passion that had come from Alice, but it was even more likely that something outside the cave had disturbed them.

Like the gang of owlhoots looking for him and Alice.

Longarm sat up abruptly, forcing Alice to roll off him. She opened her mouth to protest, but fell silent before saying anything when Longarm held a warning finger to his lips. He got lithely to his feet and pulled his trousers up, then bent down to retrieve the Winchester. He'd left a cartridge in the chamber when he laid it down the night before, so he didn't have to work the lever to make it ready to fire. Quietly, he slipped toward the mouth of the cave. He glanced behind him and saw that Alice was hurriedly dressing.

The birds were still silent. Longarm leaned toward the opening, listening for hoofbeats, footsteps, the clink of metal against rock, anything that would give him an idea of what—or who—was out there.

He didn't expect what he heard instead.

Singing floated through the air.

It wasn't particularly good singing either. A voice that cracked on seemingly every other note bellowed out, "Oh, the moon shines tonight on purty red wings! On purty red wings! On purty red wings! Oh, the moon shines tonight on purty red wings—" The singing stopped abruptly, but the same distinctive voice continued. "Whoa there, yuh danged jug-eared varmints! Whoa there, I say!"

Only when the voice stopped did Longarm become aware of the creaking of wagon wheels and the plodding of hoofbeats. The singing and then the yelling had drowned them out before. Was there a road around here? Longarm asked himself. It was entirely possible, he decided. Last night, he and Alice had been concerned only with finding a place to hide from Egan. They had no way of knowing what was in the vicinity of the cave.

Longarm moved up into the mouth of the cave so that he could see a pine-covered valley spread out in front of him. There was no road down there, at least not that he could see. But then he heard the man ask, "What the hell's the matter with yuh? Pick up a rock in your shoe?" He realized the voice was coming from above him.

Longarm leaned out and twisted his head. The slope continued for another twenty feet or so above the cave, then leveled off abruptly to form a ledge. Sitting up there on a trail that no doubt followed the ledge was a wagon with a canvas cover over its back. From where he was, Longarm couldn't see the man who was talking, but he spotted the high crown of a battered old hat moving around the team of mules hitched to the wagon.

With any luck, this was the answer to the dilemma of how he and Alice were going to get back to Virginia City. Longarm motioned for Alice to stay put, then started up the slope. He headed for the back of the wagon. When he reached the broad ledge, he slipped behind the vehicle and circled it. Just as he did so, the stranger came around the front of the team and stopped dead in his tracks. Longarm couldn't blame the man for being surprised at the unexpected sight of a burly, bare-chested man pointing a rifle at him.

"Stand easy, old son," Longarm said. "I ain't out to cause nobody any trouble."

The wagoneer was an elderly, diminutive man in a flannel shirt and buckskin pants. The brim of his hat was turned up in front. A long red mustache hung down around his mouth, and his jaw was bristly with several days' worth of beard stubble. A holster on his hip sagged from the weight of an old-fashioned, long-barreled hogleg.

"Who in tarnation are you?" he demanded. If he was afraid of Longarm, he didn't show it.

"Name's Long. I know it don't look much like it right now, but I'm a lawman. United States deputy marshal."

"Well, I'll swan. Dag-nab badge-toter, are yuh? Might's well put down that repeater, sonny. I ain't no desperado."

Longarm lowered the Winchester a little, but he kept the barrel pointing toward the man. "What are you doing up here, old-timer?"

"Headed for Virginny City to make my fortune, that's what. Gonna get me some o' the big bonanza. I got to Californy too late durin' the Gold Rush, but I ain't goin' to miss out on this'un."

A prospector. Longarm should have known. He relaxed

a little more. "What's in the wagon?" he asked, inclining his head toward the vehicle.

"All my gear. All I got in the world. Pulled up stakes back in Pennsylvania, I did, and lit a shuck for Nevada. My gran'daughter tried to talk me outta leavin', but I wouldn't hear of it, no, sir. I been sorta livin' with her an' her family the last few years, since my wife up an' died on me."

Longarm finally let the rifle barrel droop toward the ground. He had the old-timer pegged now. Just an old man trying to recapture some of the excitement of his youth. Longarm wondered if the man's granddaughter even knew where he had run off to.

At the moment, that didn't matter. What was important was that he and Alice now had a way to get back to Virginia City.

"They call me Sam," the old man said. He stepped toward Longarm and offered a gnarled hand.

Longarm shook with him and said, "You reckon you could give me and a friend a ride into Virginia City, Sam?"

"Don't see why not. Where is this friend o' yours?"

Longarm spotted Alice peeking out from behind a bush at the edge of the trail. She hadn't followed his orders to stay put this time, but he supposed he couldn't blame her for being curious, especially when it had become obvious that there wasn't going to be any shooting. He motioned for her to come out of hiding, and she stepped up onto the ledge.

The old man's eyes widened at the sight of a beautiful young blonde coming out of the bushes. Alice was dressed now, of course, but even disheveled and with her hair uncombed, she was stunning.

"Tarnation!" exclaimed Sam. "This here's your friend, Marshal?"

"That's right," Longarm said.

"Yuh got good taste in pards, that's all I can say." Sam swept his battered old hat off his bald head. "Howdy, ma'am."

173

"Hello," Alice said shyly.

Longarm made the introductions. "Alice, this is Sam. Sam, meet Alice. You two get to know each other while I go get the rest of my gear."

He slid down the slope to the cave, went inside, and put on his shirt before gathering up everything else he'd left in there. He buckled his gun belt on, settled his Stetson on his head, and carried his vest and coat as he climbed back to the road.

He found Sam and Alice sitting side by side on the wagon seat. The old man jerked a thumb over his shoulder and said, "Sorry, sonny, but you're goin' to have to ride in the back. Purty gal always gets to ride up front. Them's the rules."

Longarm chuckled and climbed in the back. Right now, he didn't mind. It would give him a chance to do some thinking.

Because something had occurred to him a few minutes earlier, something important that had almost slipped his mind when he heard the unexpected singing.

Almost . . . but not quite.

Chapter 17

Sam seemed to know where he was going. He followed the narrow road that twisted and turned through the mountains, talking all the while to Alice. Longarm sat in the back of the wagon with one of the canvas flaps lifted so that he could see out. He kept a close watch on the pine-covered slopes around them and the trail behind them, just in case Egan and the other outlaws came along.

While he rode, Longarm thought about the idea that had come to him. It was pretty far-fetched, he knew, but it cast a whole new light on everything that had happened, and in that light some things made sense that hadn't before.

The only problem with the theory was that he no longer knew what to make of Alice.

There was only one way to get to the bottom of this, and that was to get everybody together back in Virginia City and hash it all out. So Longarm was glad when he saw the towering slopes of Mount Davidson up ahead and knew they were close to the boomtown settlement.

"This must be the place," Sam announced a short time later as he brought the wagon to a stop in front of the Virginia City Opera House. The Truckee Hotel was right down the street. The old man looked around, his rheumy eyes shining with excitement. "Bein' a prospector again'll sure beat hell outta shootin' rabbits outta my gran'daughter's garden."

Longarm hopped lithely from the wagon, helped Alice climb down from the seat, and then extended his hand to Sam. "We're much obliged for the ride, old son," he said. "I'd be glad to pay you. . . ."

"Shoot, no," Sam said without hesitation. "It was payment enough just havin' a pretty lady to talk to for a while."

"I enjoyed it too," Alice told him with a smile.

Longarm took her arm and walked to the hotel with her. As they approached the building, Longarm saw two men stand up from chairs on the front porch and walk off hurriedly. He got a good enough look at them to recognize them, however—the railroad detectives, Hartley and Borden. The two men went around the corner of the hotel and disappeared.

Longarm thought about going after them, then decided that could wait. The first thing he wanted to do was let Sir Harry and Dumont know that Alice was safe.

They went inside the hotel and up to the second floor. Longarm knocked on the door of Sir Harry's suite. It was jerked open quickly, but not by the Englishman. Phillippe Dumont stood there, and when he saw Alice his eyes widened and a smile of amazement and joy spread across his face.

"Cherie!" he cried as he sprang forward and embraced Alice. "You have come back to me! You are safe, no?"

"Yes, I'm fine, Phillippe," Alice said as she tried gently to disengage herself from his octopuslike hug.

Longarm saw that Sir Harry had been lying down. The Englishman rolled to the edge of the bed and stood up, an anxious expression on his face. "Alice!" he said in a choked voice. "Are . . . are you all right, my dear?"

"I'm fine," repeated Alice. "Thanks to Marshal Long here."

That distracted Dumont and got him to let her go. Instead, before Longarm could stop him, he had thrown his arms around the big lawman. While babbling in French, Dumont kissed Longarm on both sides of his beard-stubbled face.

"Hold on there, damn it!" Longarm said as he pushed Dumont away. "I've hauled off and clouted fellas for less than that. The only reason I ain't doing that right now is because I know you got an excitable nature. Just don't try it again, old son."

Sir Harry hugged Alice, patting her on the back as he did so. He looked over her shoulder at Longarm and said, "Thank you, Marshal. Thank you from the bottom of my heart. I never meant for Alice to be hurt."

Longarm believed that, all right—just not much of anything else Sir Harry had told him.

"How in the world did you ever get her away from Egan?"

"By risking his own life, Uncle," Alice said. "Marshal Long was very valorous."

Longarm shrugged off the praise. "I been tussling with owlhoots for a long time," he said.

"What about Egan?" asked Sir Harry. "Is he dead?"

"Not that I know of."

Sir Harry frowned, clearly troubled by that news. "Then, if Egan is still at large, he may make another attempt to cause trouble for us."

"He might," Longarm agreed dryly.

Before he could say anything else, the hotel room door opened without anyone knocking on it first. Matthew Griffin strode into the room, followed by his two bodyguards and the railroad detectives, Hartley and Borden. One of the bodyguards was carrying a small carpetbag. "Marshal Long," Griffin greeted Longarm. "I heard that you were back in town."

Longarm glanced at Hartley and Borden. It had taken him a while to figure out that the railroad they worked for had a very substantial stockholder named Matthew Griffin. Clearly, the two men were aware of that fact and were eager to curry favor with the financier.

"Do you have the Golden Goddess?" Griffin went on.

"Nope," Longarm said. "I figured it was more important to rescue Miss Channing first."

"Blast it, Marshal," Griffin said impatiently, "I thought you were going to try to recover the statue."

"No need," said Longarm. "You've already got it."

That simple statement made everyone else in the room look at him in surprise, as he had expected it might. Everyone except Griffin.

The financier grinned and said, "Figured that out, did you?"

"What's the meaning of this?" Sir Harry blustered. "Are you saying, Marshal, that this man has had the Golden Goddess all along?"

"He's had the statue I took out there to Three Pines yesterday evening," Longarm said. "I'm pretty sure Hartley and Borden were part of the bunch that horned in on the ransom exchange, and it wouldn't surprise me a bit if those two were in on it too." He nodded toward Griffin's silent bodyguards.

"Wait just a minute," Hartley said. "You can't go around accusing us of . . . of . . ."

"Ambushing me and Egan and Nickerson while I was trying to trade them the statue for Miss Alice?" Longarm grinned bleakly. "That's exactly what I'm saying, old son. One of you put a bullet through Nickerson's brain. Now, by itself, that ain't no great loss. But you came damned close to ventilating me, and you could've got Miss Alice killed too." Longarm's eyes bored into Griffin's. "But you didn't care about that, did you? You just wanted to get your hands on the statue without having to pay for it."

Griffin shrugged. "When I set my sights on something, no matter what it is, I don't like having it stolen out from under me."

"So it wasn't the money?" asked Longarm.

"Oh, good Lord, no!" Griffin waved a hand toward Sir Harry. "I just didn't want that fat mountebank to think that he had gotten the better of me."

Sir Harry sputtered and started toward Griffin, but Longarm held up a hand to stop him. "Worked out mighty nice for you when Egan and Nickerson kidnapped the gal, didn't it? That way your men could bushwhack us and grab the statue in the confusion of all that lead flying around."

"I take advantage of opportunities that present themselves to me," Griffin said coldly. "How do you think I got to be a rich man? But don't blame me for what those outlaws did. I never heard of Egan or . . . what did you say his name was, Nickerson? . . . until I got here to Virginia City." He leaned his head toward Hartley and Borden. "These two filled me in on what was going on."

"This is outrageous!" Sir Harry said. "I'm going to file charges against you, sir—"

"Oh, shut up, you fat windbag," snapped Griffin. "No matter what I've admitted here in the privacy of this hotel room, you can't prove any of it."

"The testimony of a federal lawman might carry a little weight," Longarm pointed out.

"Perhaps . . . but not enough." Griffin shook his head. "No, Marshal, I'm afraid that any jury you could impanel in Nevada or California would accept my word over yours. My lawyers would see to that."

"You mean you'd bribe everybody in sight."

"I told you," Griffin said, "I like to win." He slipped a cigar from his vest pocket. "I'm curious about one thing, however. How did you figure out I was responsible for stealing the Golden Goddess?"

"You told me," Longarm said. "When you said something about that dimple on the statue's rump, I figured the only way you could know about that was if you'd seen it with your own eyes." Longarm looked at Blackstreet. "You didn't tell him about it, did you, Sir Harry?"

"No. No, I didn't." Sir Harry's voice rose a little with excitement. "There's your proof, right there! Arrest that man, Marshal!"

Griffin frowned. Obviously, the fact that he had made a little slip bothered him. But he said scornfully, "That's not

179

enough to convince anyone of anything. I might have found out about the dimple some other way."

"Nope, you've seen the statue," Longarm said with conviction. "Too bad you didn't look at it a mite closer, though."

"What the hell do you mean by that?"

"Maybe you would have noticed that the one you've got is a fake too," Longarm said mildly.

"A fake!" The exclamation came from Sir Harry, Griffin, and Phillippe Dumont, all at one. Dumont went on. "That cannot be. I told you, I switched the statues. You took the real one with you, Marshal."

Longarm shook his head patiently. "Nope. The one I took out to Three Pines wasn't the real thing either."

Griffin turned sharply to the bodyguard who was still holding the carpetbag. "Get it out," he snarled. "Let's see it."

The bodyguard opened the bag, reached inside, and brought out a paper-wrapped shape that Longarm recognized. He wasn't surprised that Griffin had brought what he considered to be the real Golden Goddess to the hotel with him. It would have pleased Griffin to watch Sir Harry squirm, knowing all the while that the statue was in the bag.

Griffin ripped away the paper around the statue, having trouble with it because his hands had started to shake. "This is the real thing," he said. "It has to be."

Longarm just shook his head solemnly. "Instead of busting it apart like Dumont did with the other one, why don't you just try scraping some of the gold off?" he suggested.

Griffin took out a small knife he probably used to cut the ends off cigars. He used the little blade to pare a sliver of gold from the shoulder of the statue. Underneath it was the gleam of more gold, and Longarm had a bad moment when it looked as if the elaborate theory he had worked out was going to be proven wrong.

But then Griffin sliced deeper with the knife, and the dull dark gray of lead appeared. "Damn it!" Griffin burst out.

He began hacking at the figurine with the knife. More and more streaks of gray began to be visible under the thin coating of gold. Griffin looked up, his face haggard. "It's a fake!"

"Yep," said Longarm.

Griffin dropped the statue. It landed on the floor with a thud. At the same time, the financier's hand snaked under his coat and came out holding a small pistol. His bodyguards must have known what was about to happen, because they produced guns too, their hands flicking under their coats to do so.

Longarm might have beaten all three of them to the draw, but he didn't want to start a gunfight in these close quarters. He stood tensely, waiting to see what was going to happen.

Griffin pointed the pistol toward a wide-eyed Sir Harry Blackstreet and rasped, "Damn you, where is it? Where's the real Golden Goddess? I want it!"

Sir Harry's mouth opened and closed several times before he was able to say, "I . . . I don't . . ."

Longarm said, "He doesn't have it."

"Then where is it?" Griffin practically snarled at him. "Who has it?"

"Nobody," said Longarm. "There isn't any Golden Goddess. There never was."

Dumont, who seemed to be just as confused as the rest of them, said, "But . . . but how . . . ?"

Longarm found himself a little glad to see that Dumont hadn't been in on the scheme. The Frenchman could be downright annoying at times, but Longarm sort of liked him in spite of that.

A dull look of resignation had come over Sir Harry's face. Alice just seemed embarrassed. Longarm looked at her and said, "Why don't you tell it, since if there's a real Golden Goddess, it's you."

Dumont looked at her. *"Cherie?"* he asked in a quavering voice.

"Oh, all right," Alice said. "I'm sorry you got mixed up in this, Phillippe. And you, Custis . . ." Her voice softened.

"I truly apologize for the danger in which you found yourself."

"You were in just as much danger as I was," Longarm told her.

Alice turned to the financier and said, "I'm sorry, Mr. Griffin, but the whole thing was a hoax. I . . . I posed for the Golden Goddess." She indicated the statue Griffin had dropped on the floor. "That one. The one you were supposed to buy from my uncle."

"But . . . but the story about the curse . . . and all the people who were after the statue . . ." Griffin was starting to look sick.

"Simply a story, deliberately spread by my uncle and the intermediaries he hired to make sure you would hear about the Golden Goddess and want it. You see, he knew of your reputation as an avid collector of antiquities . . . and of your wealth."

Griffin looked at Sir Harry and said, "But what about all the people who tried to steal it while you were on your way out here?"

"What better way to convince you the dingus was real than to have other folks seem to be after it too?" said Longarm. "That's why Sir Harry brought Nickerson in on the deal. They were partners."

"Some of the men who tried to get their hands on the statue were killed," Griffin said. "What about that?"

"They were just gunmen hired by Nickerson. He didn't care if they got killed or not, as long as the attempts on Sir Harry and Alice looked real."

Dumont sputtered, "But Alice could have been hurt too, and for that matter, so could Sir Harry!"

"The chance for great wealth sometimes requires that risks be run," Sir Harry said. "But I never meant for Alice to come to any harm, I swear that."

Griffin shook his head. "I still don't understand. What about this outlaw Egan?"

"Nickerson partnered up with him to pull off the kidnapping," said Longarm. "That was just one more thing to convince you the statue was real, Griffin. If Nickerson had lived, the switch would have gone off just fine, and then Nickerson would have brought the Goddess back here to Sir Harry, who would have sold it to you. That would have given Sir Harry and Nickerson plenty of money to pay off Egan and his men for their part, and they would have split the rest of the loot." Longarm glanced at Blackstreet. "Is that about the way it was supposed to go, Sir Harry?"

"Yes," the Englishman admitted. "And it would have worked too, if . . . if Griffin hadn't been such a bloody treacherous bastard!"

Angrily, Griffin lifted his gun. "Treacherous!" he repeated. "*You* tried to swindle *me*!"

"Griffin!" Longarm said sharply. "Listen to me, blast it! Nobody's been killed so far except Nickerson, some of the gunmen he hired, and a few of Egan's bunch. No great loss, any of 'em. Maybe it ain't quite legal, but I reckon you and your boys ought to just put those guns up and walk away from here. Let it go, Griffin."

Griffin's gaze flicked around the room. While he was considering Longarm's words, Hartley spoke up. "Mr. Griffin, I think the marshal is right. Nobody cares about those outlaws, but if you start gunning down anybody else . . ."

Longarm saw reason starting to overcome rage in Griffin's eyes. The man hadn't gotten what he wanted, but he had been saved from making a fool of himself and spending a fortune for a worthless hunk of lead. Slowly, Griffin began to lower his gun. "All right," he said. "But I'm damned if I like it—"

Longarm started to relax, and that was when Harp Egan kicked the hotel room door open and came in with both guns leveled.

"Steal that gal from me, will you!" he bellowed. "Where's that damned statue?"

Thoughts flashed through Longarm's mind. Egan must have figured when he lost their trail that he and Alice would head back to Virginia City. He had come after them, bound and determined to get his hands on the ransom he had been promised by Nickerson. Egan had no idea that there wasn't a real Golden Goddess.

But there sure as hell wasn't time to explain it all to him now, because Griffin's bodyguards, with guns already in their hands, reacted instinctively to the new threat and started throwing lead at Egan. The burly outlaw threw himself to the side and began blazing away, firing both guns as fast as he could pull the triggers.

Dumont flung himself at Alice, wrapping his arms around her and carrying her to the floor. Sir Harry took one step forward and then stopped, grunting in pain. He looked down at his chest and saw the flower of blood blossoming on his white shirtfront. Hartley and Borden both went down in the fusillade from Egan's guns. Matthew Griffin just stood there, seemingly stunned, as lead whined around his head.

Longarm palmed out his Colt, but before he could fire, he looked over Egan's shoulder and saw Sheriff Reese appear behind the outlaw. Longarm couldn't see the Greener in the lawman's hands, but he heard the roar of both barrels and saw the grisly result as the buckshot fired at close range practically blew Egan in half. Egan's corpse flopped onto the floor at Griffin's feet, blown there by the impact of the shotgun's double blast.

For a change during one of these ruckuses, Longarm hadn't fired a shot.

As the echoes died away, Alice pulled herself free of Dumont's arms and scrambled on hands and knees over to Sir Harry, who had toppled onto his back like a falling tree. He was breathing loudly and raggedly, and blood trickled out of both corners of his mouth. He lifted a hand and pawed at the air with it as if he couldn't see. "Alice?" he said weakly. "Alice . . . ?"

She caught hold of his hand and said, "I'm here, Uncle. I'm here."

Longarm holstered his gun and figured he had misjudged the two of them. It looked like Alice wasn't Sir Harry's mistress after all.

Sheriff Reese prodded Egan's corpse with a boot toe. "Couldn't believe it when I saw him ridin' down the street big as day," the lawman grunted. "I went right to fetch my old scattergun."

"Got here just in time with it too," said Longarm.

He turned back toward Sir Harry and Alice in time to hear the Englishman say in a rasping whisper, "I . . . I'm so sorry . . . never meant for you to . . . be harmed in any way . . ."

Tears were running down Alice's cheeks. "I know you didn't, Uncle," she said. "Please, don't worry about me. Just lie still, and someone can bring a physician—"

"No need," Sir Harry said. "Too late . . . for that. I saw enough men wounded . . . in the Crimea . . . know that I'm . . . done for . . ." He lifted his hand and touched her face with his fingers. "Alice . . . dear Alice . . ."

His hand fell back limply, and Alice began to sob harder. Phillippe Dumont knelt beside her, slipping an arm around her shoulders. He didn't try to pull her away from her uncle's body, just stayed there with her and held her.

Longarm turned away and saw Matthew Griffin still standing there. He appeared to be unhurt, as did his two bodyguards. The railroad detectives, Hartley and Borden, were both sitting up against the wall. Hartley had taken a slug through the left thigh, and Borden's right arm had been shattered by a bullet above the elbow. Longarm figured both of them would live, though.

"I'll fetch the doc," Sheriff Reese said. He left the room.

Griffin swallowed and looked around. "What . . . what do I do?"

Longarm picked up the worthless Golden Goddess Griffin had dropped a few minutes earlier and handed it to the financier, shoving it a little harder than absolutely necessary into Griffin's belly. "Take what you came for," Longarm told him coldly, "and go the hell back to San Francisco."

Billy Vail shoved the papers away disgustedly and said, "If this report makes a lick of sense, I sure don't see it."

Longarm lit a cheroot, blew a smoke ring, and said, "Sure it makes sense. You just got to remember that almost everybody mixed up in the whole mess was either a liar, a swindler, or an owlhoot."

Vail pointed a pudgy finger at Longarm's report. "What about this? There wasn't ever a real Golden Goddess?"

"Nope. Alice told me later that the one that was supposed to be real was sculpted by an Englishman named Haversham. Sir Harry paid him to do it, and Alice modeled for the statue. She enjoyed it so much that when Dumont asked her to pose for him later, she went along with it."

"How in blazes did you know she posed for the Golden Goddess?"

"The dimple." Longarm took another puff on the cheroot.

"What dimple?" asked Vail, an edge of desperation creeping into his voice.

"The dimple on Alice's rear end. There was one just like it on the statue."

Vail took a deep breath and pressed his palms down hard on the top of his desk. "I've seen a few naked women in my time, Custis," he said slowly. "More than one of them had a damned dimple on her butt!"

Longarm sat up straighter in the red leather chair and cleared his throat. "Yeah, but, I, uh, did some studying and comparing—"

The chief marshal held up both hands to stop him. "All right, all right, I'll take your word for it. You turned out to be right, so I reckon that's all that matters." Vail shuffled some more of the papers. "I see here you let Miss Channing and that Dumont fellow go on back to England. The woman could've been charged with being an accessory to fraud."

"Attempted fraud," Longarm pointed out. "And that ain't a federal charge, Billy. Sheriff Reese there in Virginia City didn't want her, so I figured the best thing would be to let her and Dumont go on home." Longarm grinned. "Dumont's still figuring on finishing up that statue of Alice he was sculpting. You know, for somebody who was supposed to be more fond of fellas than gals, Dumont seemed awful friendly toward Alice."

"I don't want to hear about any of that either," Vail said crisply. "Was Blackstreet really a British nobleman?"

"Yep. A hero in the Crimean War too, just like he claimed. And a pretty rich man at one time, until he had a run of bad luck. But he didn't own part of a mine in Nevada or anything like that. That was just part of the story he spread around so people would think the Golden Goddess was real."

Vail sighed and said grudgingly, "All right, I reckon it all hangs together if you squint your eyes and look at it just right. It beats the hell out of me how you keep on getting mixed up in things like this, though. Being a deputy marshal used to be a simple job."

Longarm couldn't recall when his job had been all that simple, but he didn't point that out to Vail. Instead he stood up and said, "Well, if you don't need for anything else, Billy . . ."

"Hold on. Who said I didn't have another job for you?"

Longarm tried not to groan. "I just got back from Virginia City."

"Well, I'm not sending you back to Nevada. It just so happens there's a chore down in Texas needs some tending to. Something about a bunch of cattle that keeps getting stolen and then brought back." Vail grinned evilly. "And while you're down there, you can see if there are any dimples on those cows' butts!"

Watch for

LONGARM AND THE SINS OF SISTER SIMONE

262nd novel in the exciting LONGARM series
from Jove

Coming in September!